THE WINNING POST IS LOVE

The Marquis stirred and then realised he had been asleep.

As he opened his eyes, something soft and gentle against his shoulder murmured,

"Oh, Euan darling, if only we could always be like this, how wonderful life would be!"

He had heard women say those same words many times and quite suddenly and for no particular reason, it irritated him.

He did not answer and an arm went round his neck.

It was only with the greatest difficulty he did not fight it off.

He did not really understand it himself, but this had happened to him before.

Quite unexpectedly, he was tired of the liaison that had seemed so exciting and now he wanted only to be free.

'Free' was indeed perhaps the right word.

THE BARBARA CARTLAND PINK COLLECTION

Titles in this series

THE WINNING POST IS LOVE

BARBARA CARTLAND

Barbaracartland.com Ltd

THE BARBARA CARTLAND PINK COLLECTION

Dame Barbara Cartland is still regarded as the most prolific bestselling author in the history of the world.

In her lifetime she was frequently in the Guinness Book of Records for writing more books than any other living author.

Her most amazing literary feat was to double her output from 10 books a year to over 20 books a year when she was 77 to meet the huge demand.

She went on writing continuously at this rate for 20 years and wrote her very last book at the age of 97, thus completing an incredible 400 books between the ages of 77 and 97.

Her publishers finally could not keep up with this phenomenal output, so at her death in 2000 she left behind an amazing 160 unpublished manuscripts, something that no other author has ever achieved.

Barbara's son, Ian McCorquodale, together with his daughter Iona, felt that it was their sacred duty to publish all these titles for Barbara's millions of admirers all over the world who so love her wonderful romances.

So in 2004 they started publishing the 160 brand new Barbara Cartlands as *The Barbara Cartland Pink Collection*, as Barbara's favourite colour was always pink – and yet more pink!

The Barbara Cartland Pink Collection is published monthly exclusively by Barbaracartland.com and the books are numbered in sequence from 1 to 160.

Enjoy receiving a brand new Barbara Cartland book each month by taking out an annual subscription to the Pink Collection, or purchase the books individually.

The Pink Collection is available from the Barbara Cartland website www.barbaracartland.com via mail order and through all good bookshops.

In addition Ian and Iona are proud to announce that The Barbara Cartland Pink Collection is now available in ebook format as from Valentine's Day 2011.

For more information, please contact us at:

Barbaracartland.com Ltd.
Camfield Place
Hatfield
Hertfordshire AL9 6JE
United Kingdom

Telephone: +44 (0)1707 642629
Fax: +44 (0)1707 663041
Email: info@barbaracartland.com

THE LATE DAME BARBARA CARTLAND

Barbara Cartland who sadly died in May 2000 at the age of nearly 99 was the world's most famous romantic novelist who wrote 723 books in her lifetime with worldwide sales of over 1 billion copies and her books were translated into 36 different languages.

As well as romantic novels, she wrote historical biographies, 6 autobiographies, theatrical plays, books of advice on life, love, vitamins and cookery. She also found time to be a political speaker and television and radio personality.

She wrote her first book at the age of 21 and this was called *Jigsaw*. It became an immediate bestseller and sold 100,000 copies in hardback and was translated into 6 different languages. She wrote continuously throughout her life, writing bestsellers for an astonishing 76 years. Her books have always been immensely popular in the United States, where in 1976 her current books were at numbers 1 & 2 in the B. Dalton bestsellers list, a feat never achieved before or since by any author.

Barbara Cartland became a legend in her own lifetime and will be best remembered for her wonderful romantic novels, so loved by her millions of readers throughout the world.

Her books will always be treasured for their moral message, her pure and innocent heroines, her good looking and dashing heroes and above all her belief that the power of love is more important than anything else in everyone's life.

"Over many years I have written so much about love and, please always remember, the wonder of love never diminishes with age. On the contrary love grows stronger and deeper and stays with you in this life and in the many lives yet to come."

Barbara Cartland

CHAPTER ONE
1859

Lord Waincliffe took his horse at a very high jump.

He was delighted when Starlight cleared it without any difficulty.

At the same time, when Starlight threw his head up, pleased as he was at his prowess, Lord Waincliffe saw that the bridle was almost broken in one place.

Knowing it would be dangerous to ride such a high-spirited animal if the bridle broke, he looked for help.

To his relief he could see just ahead of him a pretty house and then he remembered it had been let by his father on a very long lease to a University Professor, whose name was Peter Stourton.

He rode carefully towards the house.

As he drew near, he saw that on the lawn in front of it there was a girl bathing a small dog.

Believing that it would be risky to continue riding in case the bridle broke completely, he called out,

"Excuse me, but can you possibly help me?"

The girl then looked up, smiled and walked towards him.

"Good morning, my Lord, I saw you go by just now and thought what a splendid horse you were riding."

"You are Rosetta Stourton, are you not?"

"Yes, I am Rosetta, my Lord."

"Starlight has just taken the highest jump I could find for him, but unfortunately his bridle looks likely to break at any minute and I will then have very little control over him."

The girl gave a cry.

"I will go and find what you need, my Lord, and I should stay where you are, mounted on him, otherwise he might become restless and break the bridle completely."

"That is just what I thought myself and thank you very much," replied Lord Waincliffe.

The girl ran into the house and he patted Starlight to keep him calm and quiet until she returned.

She was even quicker than he expected and came running out with some special tape he recognised at once as being sticky on one side – he had used it himself on fishing rods.

She seemed breathless when she reached him and he stretched out to take it from her, saying,

"Thank you very much, I am most grateful."

"Let me help you, my Lord, I can do it more easily standing here than you could sitting on the saddle."

She wound the tape round the bridle and then cut it with a pair of scissors she had brought with her.

"I'm sorry to have interrupted you when you are so busy," he murmured politely. "I hope your dog will not dirty himself again while you are attending to me."

"I don't think he has wandered far away."

Then she stood back and added,

"I'm sure this will hold firm at least until you reach home."

Lord Waincliffe looked at her.

He thought that she was exceedingly pretty and she reminded him of someone.

Then he was aware that she was very much like his sister Dolina and in fact, there was a remarkable likeness and he reflected that if they were side by side it would be difficult to know which was which.

"I am extremely grateful to you, Miss Stourton," he said aloud. "I hope your father is well."

"He finds it extremely annoying that his eyesight is failing. Although I read to him as much as I can, he prefers to 'explore a book' as he calls it, himself."

Lord Waincliffe laughed.

"I know exactly what he means. You must tell him how sorry I am that he has this affliction, which affects so many older people. I shall doubtless suffer from it myself when I am his age."

"Papa is wonderful in other ways. He can garden, which he loves, and exercise our dogs in your beautiful woods."

Lord Waincliffe hesitated before he exclaimed,

"Please keep them under control! You know I shall want to enjoy my shooting in the autumn."

"I promise you they behave very well, my Lord. They are model dogs and other people could learn a great deal from them if they could see how obedient they are."

"Thank you again and I will now take Starlight home without being afraid I might lose control of him."

"He is a beautiful horse," she sighed, as she patted him. "I am not at all surprised that you are proud of his appearance apart from his skill."

"I think he will be the best jumper I have ever had."

Lord Waincliffe raised his hat.

Then, as he rode off on Starlight, he was thinking how extremely pretty Professor Stourton's daughter was.

It was strange that she should be so like his sister.

He rode towards his house, which had been in the Waincliffe family for generations.

He was thinking, as he had so often thought before, how much needed doing to it. Yet it was impossible for him and his brother to find any money to spend on it.

The sun was shimmering on the windows and it made the pink of the Elizabethan bricks of its façade look even more attractive than usual.

'I do love my home,' Lord Waincliffe mused, as he drew nearer.

He hoped as he had hoped a thousand times already that the scheme he and his brother were currently planning would materialise.

When he reached the stables, the old groom came hurrying towards him.

"Did you 'ave a good ride, my Lord?" he asked.

"Splendid! Starlight jumped even better than I ever anticipated, Brown. But then he nearly broke his bridle."

"There now, I shouldn't 'ave given you that 'un. I noticed yesterday it were crackin', so to speak, and now I see you've 'ad to bind it up."

"I asked Professor Stourton's daughter to do it for me, but I hope you will be able to mend it properly."

"There be a saddle-maker in the next village. I'll take it to 'im, but 'e be gettin' a bit older and it takes 'im longer than it used to."

Lord Waincliffe did not answer Brown.

He dismounted and after patting Starlight, he turned and walked towards the house.

He was thinking that there were so many things in the stables in urgent need of repair and indeed several of the mangers needed completely replacing.

'It's all a question of money,' he told himself, 'but I am sure that, if only the Marquis will collaborate with us, we shall make a fortune from the Racecourse.'

He walked in through the front door.

Because he was economising, there was not the liveried footman there used to be in the hall to take his hat and whip.

He threw them down on a chair and went into the study. It was a most comfortable and cosy room where his brother and sister sat unless they had visitors.

There were some fine pictures on the walls, but the sofa and armchairs needed recovering and the curtains over the windows were deeply faded.

As Lord Waincliffe entered the study, his brother, Henry, looked up from the writing table.

"Oh, you are back, Gordon! How did you get on?"

"Starlight went like a dream," his brother answered, "but I nearly had an accident as his bridle was on the point of breaking."

"That was dangerous," remarked Henry.

"It could well have been, but I stopped at Professor Stourton's house and his daughter, Rosetta, kindly stuck it together for me so that I could ride home safely."

"I suppose it will have to be repaired, but I am certain that saddler in the next village overcharges us."

"I'd expect he is in need of money as much as we are," Lord Waincliffe replied. "But the Marquis is coming this evening and I am just keeping my fingers crossed."

"So am I," said Henry. "But if he refuses to help with the Racecourse, what shall we do, Gordon?"

"I will face that jump when I come to it, but at the moment I am exhausted and very thirsty. Is there anything to drink in the house?"

"There is always water," Henry said mischievously, "and, of course beer, which the servants always drink as their right."

His brother made a grimace.

"What I would really like," he muttered, "is a glass of champagne."

Henry laughed.

"'*If wishes were horses then beggars might ride!*' You know as well as I do the cellar is empty."

"When I think how full it was in our grandfather's day, I feel like crying."

"I daresay cook has a lemon in the kitchen. Shall I tell her to make you some lemonade?"

"Don't bother," his brother answered, "I will wait until luncheon. I think her lemonade is rather nasty."

"Just as you please," Henry replied. "But we will need to have something for the Marquis when he arrives tonight."

"Yes, of course, and indeed I have thought of that already. I have bought some bottles of champagne and an excellent white wine. And I have purchased a bottle of the same whisky I saw him drinking the other day."

"Well, let's hope he is satisfied with that," Henry sighed.

He walked from the writing table across the room to stand in front of the fireplace.

As it was summer there was no fire and his sister had therefore put a pot of geraniums in the fireplace and they gave a touch of colour to the room.

Because the Marquis was coming to dinner tonight, Dolina had arranged flowers in front of the windows.

There was no point in opening the drawing room for just one guest.

Besides the designs for the Racecourse the brothers hoped to build were in the study laid out on a table against one of the walls.

Gordon was thinking he would have another look at them when the door opened.

His sister came in.

Dolina was very beautiful and had been acclaimed in London as one of the beauties of the Season.

That had happened last year when she had been presented at Court and this year they had not been able to afford to open the London house.

As Dolina entered, the two brothers looked at her in surprise.

She was dressed in one of her smartest dresses and there was a blue driving cape over her shoulders. On her head was an elaborate hat trimmed with feathers.

"Where are you going?" Gordon asked. "As you are dressed up to the nines, it must be somewhere grand."

"I am going to London," replied Dolina.

"London!" Henry echoed. "But you cannot leave us. You know that the Marquis is coming here tonight."

"I really cannot help that. I have been invited by the Countess of Leamington to a big dinner party tonight and a ball at the Duchess of Devonshire's afterwards."

"You realise as well as I do," Gordon interposed, "that it all depends on *you* whether the Marquis will help us with the Racecourse or not. You know only too well that he likes pretty women."

"I have heard more than enough about that tiresome roué. He would not look at me when I was a *debutante* and it's very doubtful if he will do so now. What he likes are married women with complacent husbands."

She spoke scornfully, but Henry asserted,

"Do be sensible, Dolina. We are relying on you to amuse the Marquis and make him happy to be here. No one knows better than you do that we don't have enough money to buy ourselves a donkey, let alone new horses and build a Racecourse."

"I know. You have not talked of anything else for the last two months, but I am *not* going to miss this ball."

She tossed her head, then added in a defiant tone,

"Besides there will be someone there tonight I am very interested to see again. And he is definitely not like that tiresome Marquis and his reputation with women."

"Please listen to me – " Gordon began.

But his sister gave a little cry.

"I think I can hear the carriage. They told me they would pick me up at twelve o'clock and we are having luncheon with friends on the way."

She walked defiantly towards the door, saying,

"Goodbye boys. I wish you good luck with your Marquis, but I will be dancing, I expect, with someone far more enchanting."

She then pulled open the door before either of her brothers could move and they heard her running down the passage towards the hall.

For a brief moment, Gordon considered going after her to beg her again to stay with them.

But he knew it was hopeless.

Even as he hesitated, he could now hear a carriage moving away.

Now he thought about it, he remembered that when he came in he had seen a trunk in the hall, but he had not paid any attention.

With her, he then told himself dismally, went their chance of the Marquis helping them.

The Marquis of Millbrook had indeed, as Dolina had indicated, a very bad reputation.

He was tall, dark and handsome and had come into his title when he was only twenty-two.

He was immensely rich and owned one of the finest and most prestigious ancestral castles in the country. His very large estate adjoined their much smaller one.

It was, of course, the Marquis, who was the talk of the neighbourhood and he was noted in London for being a close friend of the Prince of Wales.

He even rivalled His Royal Highness in the number of women he chased.

It had been Gordon's idea that they should build a Racecourse.

They owned a most suitable piece of land, which adjoined the Marquis's estate and if he would collaborate with them, Gordon believed, it would be of great advantage to them both.

As they were relatively near London and within reach of several fairly large towns, it would undoubtedly be most profitable – and there was no other Racecourse anywhere near them.

But *everything* depended on the Marquis.

All that Gordon and Henry could supply was the land for the Racecourse itself and they had to be frank and admit that they could not put up any capital themselves.

Because the Marquis was famed as a roué where women were concerned, both brothers were counting on Dolina to persuade him to help them.

But, as she said, he was much more interested in older married women than he was in girls of her age, but as she was so lovely, the two brothers were convinced that the Marquis would be fascinated by her.

She would at least put him into the right frame of mind for being generous.

Now, as they looked at each other, Gordon sighed,

"Well, that's another dream gone. When I last saw the Marquis he said that he was looking forward to seeing Dolina, as he had heard she was the most beautiful girl in Mayfair."

"Who on earth could take her place?" Henry asked.

"No one," Gordon responded bluntly. "And as you well know, the girls round here are very pleasant when we meet them, but you could hardly say they are beauties."

Henry knew this to be true.

There were a few local girls, but none of them were particularly exceptional as the Marquis was expecting and there was not one to compete in any way with what Gordon had referred to as 'the Mayfair beauties.'

He walked across the room and flung himself down in a chair.

"Well, that ends yet another chance," he said again. "We may as well send a message to the Marquis to tell him not to come, rather than let him be blasé and bored, as he undoubtedly will be when he arrives."

Gordon sighed.

They had taken so much trouble buying the best wine they thought the Marquis would like and choosing the food, which the old cook, who had been with them since they were born, could do best.

They had made Barnes, the ancient butler, polish up the silver and it was now shining as brightly as he had said himself, 'as them stars.'

Then all of a sudden Gordon sat up and shouted,

"I have an idea!"

"What is that?" Henry asked without enthusiasm.

"There is a chance, just a chance, that we might be able to produce Dolina when the Marquis arrives."

Henry looked at him.

"You must be raving mad, Gordon! You know as well as I do that Dolina would not come back even if we offered her a thousand pounds."

"I did tell you that I had had trouble with Starlight's bridle and that then Professor Stourton's daughter, Rosetta, stuck it together so that I could ride home safely."

"What has that got to do with it?"

"While she was mending the bridle, I thought she was not only very pretty but that she looked extraordinarily like Dolina."

Henry chuckled.

"You are not dragging up that old story again, are you?"

"What old story?" Gordon asked in surprise.

"Oh, you must have heard it," Henry answered. "It was whispered that, when Mama was so ill and had to be in London, leaving Papa alone here, he had an *affaire-de-coeur*, if you want to put it politely, with Mrs. Stourton."

His brother stared at him.

"What are you saying?"

"You must have heard the story hundreds of times. Apparently when the Professor was at the University, his wife became bored with endless talk about undergraduates and what they knew and did not know. So she often used to come back here on her own to keep the house going. And one of her most frequent visitors was our father."

11

Gordon stared at him.

"Are you then seriously telling me, Henry, that you think Stourton's daughter, who I do admit is exceedingly pretty, is the result of a liaison between our Papa and Mrs. Stourton?"

"I heard my nanny talk about it when I was still in the nursery, but I suppose, as you were older than me, they were more careful what they said in front of you."

"I can hardly believe it!" exclaimed Gordon, "but Papa did like pretty women and Mama was constantly ill after you were born and she had to keep having treatment in London."

"Well, that is the gossip I listened to as I played with my fort and my soldiers on the nursery floor," Henry said. "I have often wanted to meet Rosetta Stourton, just to see for myself if there is any likeness to Papa."

"It's so difficult to know if a woman looks like a man," Gordon replied. "But she is certainly astonishingly like Dolina."

The two brothers stared at each other.

"I know what you are thinking," Henry remarked, "but I don't think she would do it."

"We can at least try. Let's go over there now, tell her about the Racecourse and ask her if she would act the part of Dolina and then be clever enough to deceive the Marquis."

"I think it's a crazy idea, Gordon, but it's either that or we might as well give up right away!"

Gordon nodded and Henry went on,

"There is no time to ask anyone else who is really attractive. We should have to go as far as London to find anyone pretty enough to please the Marquis."

"I just don't believe he is such a roué as they make out, but as he moves with the 'Marlborough Set' it's not surprising if he has an appetite for a real beauty."

"Which is more than we can offer him here," Henry chimed in, "where the girls all look strong and healthy, but if you ask me, they are all extremely boring."

"I think we are asking too much, but equally we either have to give up our idea of building the Racecourse, which I am certain would be a most profitable addition to the estate, or chance our luck with Rosetta Stourton."

"Well, *nothing ventured nothing gained*," muttered Henry. "I think we might at least ask her to help us. If that fails, then we will have to send a message to the Marquis saying the Racecourse idea is off. I myself would rather do that than have him tell us he is just not interested."

"We will go to her father's house after luncheon," Gordon suggested. "It's a chance in a million, but let's give it a try."

Next the door opened and Barnes announced,

"Luncheon is served, my Lord, and, if there 'aint much of it, it's 'cos me wife be busy planning the meal for tonight when his Lordship be with us."

The two brothers walked into the dining room.

They found a cold and somewhat unappetising meal awaiting them, but neither of them was particularly hungry.

As long as Barnes was in the room, they were silent and only when they had finished eating, did Gordon say,

"I know without you saying so you think I am mad. But, as it is our last and only chance, we have to be brave enough to try it."

"All right," Henry agreed. "I will just make myself look a little more respectable. We will ride there, because it always looks better if gentlemen arrive on horseback."

"That's your idea, my dear brother. Although it's a somewhat conceited one, I grant you it has a point but not a very strong one."

"Well, there is nothing else we can do," said Henry. "And I have always had the idea that women admire a man when he is mounted!"

Gordon laughed and then he added,

"Come on. Keep your wit for Rosetta Stourton and your words of consolation for when we return home having been told our idea is quite ridiculous."

"I am not going to bet on it, simply because I have no money."

"I seem to have heard that somewhere before," his brother replied, "and for Heaven's sake don't say it again."

"We will doubtless be saying it after tomorrow not once but a thousand times," Henry murmured gloomily.

Then, as they walked to the stables, he said,

"Cheer up, Gordon. If the girl refuses to help us, we will just have to think of some other way of amusing the Marquis."

"If you can do that, you are brilliant. Personally, I can think of nothing in the house he does not have better himself. Although I am extremely proud of our treasures, which are entailed on to the son I am never likely to afford, we can only say that we have done our best and no one could ask for more."

"You sound as if you are writing your obituary!"

As Gordon attempted to chastise Henry jokingly for his impertinence, they were both laughing.

There was no sign of the groom who was obviously on his break and so they saddled the horses themselves and Gordon chose a different mount from Starlight.

The one treasure they did have was a stable of well-bred horses, but there was, however, no chance of Gordon racing them as his father had managed to do.

The sun was shining and the birds were singing as they rode away from Waincliffe Hall.

As boys they had liked the Professor and had often visited him in the holidays.

Then they found they could discuss international affairs with him that were beyond their other neighbours' capabilities.

Gordon was trying to remember what Mrs. Stourton looked like.

Vaguely at the back of his mind, he thought she was very pretty, but, as he was only a boy at the time, he could not recollect her at all clearly.

They then reached the house with its flower-filled garden and where he had seen Rosetta washing her dog this morning.

As they did so, Gordon saw that she was again in the garden, but now she was sitting in a deckchair reading a newspaper.

As the two brothers pulled in their horses outside the garden gate, she looked up in surprise.

Then she put down the newspaper, rose and walked towards them.

By the time she reached them they had dismounted and were tying their horses' bridles to the wooden fence.

As she opened the gate, she called out,

"Surely you are not in trouble again?"

"In much greater trouble," replied Gordon. "We've come to ask your help, but to a very different problem from the one I brought to you this morning."

Rosetta looked a little surprised.

"Of course, I will help you if I can, but I just cannot believe that *both* those magnificent horses you have just attached to our fence have broken bridles too."

"I think," Henry said before Gordon could reply, "that it is *we* who have broken bridles and that is why we need your help."

Rosetta looked puzzled.

Henry thought, as he was looking at her, that she did closely resemble his sister.

They had the same coloured hair, the same pink and white skin and they were both gloriously pretty.

He was aware, as he looked at her, that Gordon was thinking the same.

In fact his brother was thinking that, if you put the two girls together, they might almost be twins.

They walked to where Rosetta had been sitting and she brought up two more deckchairs.

The two brothers hurried to take them from her and opened them and, as they all sat down, Rosetta said,

"Now tell me what I can do to help you, gentlemen. Of course, I should love to be able to do so, although you do make it sound particularly difficult."

"It's very difficult indeed," admitted Gordon. "We only hope you will not be shocked at what we have to say."

Rosetta opened wide her very attractive eyes and he saw they were the same colour as his sister's – not the pale blue that most people thought of as being very English, but a much deeper blue.

"Let me first tell you," Gordon began, "why we are in trouble."

"What sort of trouble?" she asked.

"Well, we are almost broke in the first place and Henry and I had a brilliant scheme to save ourselves from almost bankruptcy of building a Racecourse on our estate and adjoining land owned by our neighbour, the Marquis of Millbrook."

Rosetta looked surprise and then she exclaimed,

"That is a wonderful idea! Of course, it would be a great attraction in this part of the world, but how could you possibly afford it?"

"This is the whole point," Gordon replied. "That is why we want *your* help."

"To pay for your Racecourse?"

"No, no, of course not. Well, not in money, but in persuading the Marquis of Millbrook to help us."

There was a short pause and then she asked,

"Do you really think I could do it? He is a very strange man from what I have heard. He rarely pays any attention to anything that happens in the County."

"That is because he is always in London," Gordon said. "But I have the feeling he might find it interesting, as he is an outstanding rider, to own with us a Racecourse here right under his nose."

Rosetta gave a little laugh.

"It's certainly a marvellous idea, but I cannot see how I can help you with it."

"That is the point. The Marquis is well known for pursuing beautiful women and he finds them much more amusing than a Racecourse – "

"That is one way of putting it and, of course, I have heard about him. No one talks of anyone else in this part of the world."

"I am sure that's true," said Henry. "He is actually coming to see us this evening to talk about our idea and we are praying, as you can imagine, that he will agree and put up the money for it."

"Have you really gone as far as that?" she asked. "How wonderful and it would be great for us all to have a Racecourse so near. It would undoubtedly bring a great deal of employment to the whole neighbourhood."

"That is exactly what we thought and that is why you have to help us, because, if you don't, I think we may have to forget the Racecourse straight away."

"What do you mean by that?"

Gordon glanced at his brother as if for help before he replied slowly,

"Our sister, Dolina, who you must have met, was to have been with us tonight of all nights, when the Marquis comes to dinner to discuss the Racecourse, but she decided at the last moment to go to London."

Rosetta looked astonished.

"Go to London!" she cried. "But why particularly just now?"

"She has been invited to a special party," Gordon said, "and it was more important to her than the Marquis could ever be. I suppose we have to accept that."

"I can easily see your sister's point, but equally I do appreciate your dilemma."

"What we would love you to do, is to come and make yourself very pleasant to the Marquis, so that he does not feel he is wasting his time."

Gordon paused and Henry knew he was frightened of saying it.

"What my brother is trying to tell you is that you look exactly like our sister, Dolina, and just for dinner tonight and luncheon tomorrow we were wondering if you would be kind enough and generous enough to come and stay the night and pretend to be her."

Rosetta stared at him as if she could hardly believe what he had just said and then she asked,

"Are you serious?"

"Very serious indeed," Gordon replied. "Because the Marquis said he is looking forward to seeing her again, although she claimed he had paid no attention to her in London. At the same time as he has so many beautiful women around him, we feel it a compliment he has shown any interest in her at all."

"What is more," Henry chipped in, "if he arrives and finds she is not there and preferring to be in London, he might take considerable umbrage and then refuse to even discuss the Racecourse with us."

"I cannot believe he would do that, but I suppose he might! I have heard he is most unpredictable and not in the least like other men."

"You have never met him?" Gordon asked her.

She shook her head.

"No, but I have heard enough about him to fill a hundred books. I have never even shaken hands with him and I don't suppose he knows Papa and I even exist."

"That makes things ever better. If you will pretend to be our sister just for a few hours, then if he wants to see Dolina again, he can do so as soon as she returns home."

"Suppose he guesses that I am not your sister or I do something wrong and you are ashamed of me?"

"I am sure you will only need to be yourself. Just flatter the Marquis a little and tell him how important he is. And then enthuse that a first class Racecourse is vitally needed here and that only he can provide it."

Quite unexpectedly Rosetta laughed.

"I just don't believe that this conversation is taking place. It's like something out of a book or a dream and I will wake up and find I have imagined the whole thing."

"All we want," Gordon persisted, "is a Racecourse that will bring prosperity to the neighbourhood and which will provide endless interest for my brother and me and, we hope, considerable profit."

"Then," Henry added, "we will be able to repair the house and have money for the best horses in the stables."

"You certainly make it sound very attractive, but I am still afraid that the Marquis will not think I am nearly as beautiful as your sister and I may then be much more of a hindrance than a help."

"Are you saying you will do it?" Henry asked her eagerly.

"I think it would be rather fun, but I am frightened I may let you down and then you would never forgive me."

"We will promise not to," Gordon insisted. "If you will do this for us, we will be eternally grateful."

"Don't count the chickens before they are hatched," Henry interposed. "We will be very grateful to you just for making the effort and it will be wonderful if our idea of a Racecourse becomes a reality."

"That's so true," his brother admitted. "So please, please, Rosetta, help us. Otherwise I am quite sure that the Marquis will be bored with only Henry and me to entertain him and he will have left long before we finish telling him what our glorious Racecourse could be like."

"That would be a disaster!" she exclaimed. "I am only hoping I will not let you down. Are you quite certain that I really do look like your sister? I have been told she is very beautiful."

"You are *so* like her," Gordon said, "that it's almost uncanny."

"What we should say," Henry came in, "is that in a way you are even more beautiful than Dolina!"

There was a pause and then she enquired,

"When do you want me to come to The Hall?"

"We would like you to come literally as soon as you possibly can, and, of course, stay for the night," Gordon replied. "There are a great many things we have to tell you before the Marquis arrives so you don't make a mistake."

Rosetta nodded and he continued,

"Also it would be wise for you to wear some of Dolina's pretty gowns from London. They were actually given to her as a present by her Godmother. So they are very expensive and very smart!"

"Now you are definitely tempting me – "

"One thing you must not forget," said Henry, "is that you must always call yourself 'Dolina'."

"Certainly and I will come as soon as possible and stay the night, if that is what you want me to do."

"Your father will not mind you leaving him?"

"No, my Lord. He will be pleased that I am to see, as I have always wanted, all the lovely treasures you have in your house."

She smiled before she added,

"Actually my aunt is staying here at present and is with him now. She, I know, will keep him happy until I return."

"Then that will settle everything," declared Henry. "How can we tell you how extremely sporting it is of you? We are very very grateful."

"More grateful than we could ever put into words," echoed Gordon, "but I know when you see the Racecourse, it will be a reward in itself."

"It certainly will," agreed Rosetta. "Perhaps you will be kind enough to send a carriage for me at about four o'clock."

"It will be outside the door and please don't change your mind. We will be waiting very anxiously for you."

"I think it will be a very exciting adventure, but you will have to show me and tell me everything I will have to remember so that I don't make any silly mistakes."

"It will be a great adventure for us too," Gordon trumpeted, "and we will be waiting for you."

The brothers rose to their feet and started to walk across the lawn towards their horses.

Only when they had left the house behind and were riding back towards The Hall did Henry cry in an excited tone,

"*We have done it!* We have done it! Now we have jumped the first fence, I am certain we are going to reach the winning post!"

CHAPTER TWO

Gordon took a long time arranging the sketches for the Racecourse.

He had already done it about half a dozen times, but he was now certain he had not left out anything that would appeal to the Marquis.

He was also concerned that Rosetta Stourton should be made familiar with the house and brought up-to-date with everything they had planned for so long.

He could hardly believe, because Dolina had taken so much interest in the project that she had let them down at the very last moment.

But she had hinted to him that there was someone she particularly wanted to be with at this party.

Gordon had had a suspicion for some time that she was in love and who the man was and why he did not seem to reciprocate to anyone as beautiful as Dolina, he could not understand.

He was naturally upset that she would not be there to help them and yet he thought it unlikely that the Marquis would have the slightest idea that Rosetta Stourton was not the genuine article.

He looked round the drawing room, which Dolina had tidied before she left and thought it looked welcoming and comfortable.

It was not likely that he would impress the Marquis with The Hall when his Castle was so superior.

He knew, if he was to be frank with himself, he had always been somewhat jealous of the Marquis.

If he did not live so near and his Castle was not so overwhelming, undoubtedly Waincliffe Hall would have been the most splendid in the County.

'If we can collaborate now, it will be of tremendous help to us,' he thought. 'It will also help the County and many villages urgently need help.'

Gordon arranged that the Marquis should have the best of the State bedrooms, that had all been getting rather dilapidated and faded over the years.

It had been impossible for him and Henry to invite large parties of people to stay, as it not only cost too much money, but they did not have enough servants.

Gordon thought now that it would be appropriate for Rosetta to be in Dolina's room.

Every member of the family he had ever read about or known had been keen on horses and if only they could build their Racecourse, the stables would be full again – instead of being virtually empty as they were at present.

'This is a big gamble,' he muttered to himself, 'and if we win it will be a miracle.'

*

In her own house Rosetta was telling her aunt that she was going to Waincliffe Hall and she had been invited to stay the night for a special dinner party.

"Well, all I can say," her aunt exclaimed, "is it's about time that they asked you. I have frequently thought, considering how fond their father was of your mother, it was disgraceful the way you were ignored after she died."

"Well, they are making up for it now, Aunt Sarah, so we must not complain. I am looking forward to meeting the Marquis, who I understand will be there too."

She was very careful not to tell her aunt why the Marquis had been invited to The Hall, as she was sure that Lord Waincliffe would not wish to be pitied if the Marquis refused to do what he and his brother needed so urgently.

"If that Marquis is going to stay," her aunt said sharply, "I hope you will be properly chaperoned. From all I hear, his behaviour in London exceeds even that of the Prince of Wales!"

Rosetta laughed.

"Now, you have been listening to too much gossip, Aunt Sarah. I am certain the Marquis is not as bad as he is painted.

"I have heard enough stories about him in the last few years to fill a book, Rosetta. A good friend of mine in London has told me disgraceful things about his behaviour. You must be very careful not to become embroiled."

"That is highly unlikely, Aunt Sarah. As all those beauties in London run after him, because he is so good-looking, I hardly think he is likely to bother about me."

Her aunt did not reply and Rosetta knew that she had scored a point.

Equally it made her even more curious about the Marquis than she had been before.

Of course she had seen him, as she often went to the meet of the local foxhounds and she had seen pictures of him in *The Ladies Journal*, not that she enjoyed it very much, but her aunt read every word and knew more about London Society than she did about their local village.

Aloud she remarked,

"I do hope while I am away that you will read Papa the books he enjoys. He is not really interested in novels or hearing about modern Society."

"Who can blame him!" exclaimed Aunt Sarah.

"What he enjoys, as you know," Rosetta went on, "are books on the history of the countries he has visited."

"I know, my dear, but I find those places difficult to pronounce and to tell you the truth, the history your father enjoys I find incredibly dull!"

When Rosetta told her father where she was going, he said at once,

"That is the best piece of news I have had for some time. I have often wondered why his Lordship did not ask you to The Hall."

He was silent for a moment and then he added,

"As you going to meet the Marquis, then please ask him something I have been longing to know for years."

"What is that, Papa?"

"I want to know if the picture of Queen Elizabeth, which I understand hangs in one of the best rooms, was a contemporary portrait or painted after she was dead."

"Why should you want to know, Papa?"

"It's a portrait I always remember seeing when I was first taken round The Castle by the old Marquis and it is most certainly one of the most striking pictures in his possession and that's saying a great deal, but I have always wondered in my own mind whether it is genuine or not."

It was so like her father to let something like that trouble him, Rosetta reflected.

"I promise you I will not forget to ask the Marquis, but I do think, if you don't know the answer, then he will probably not either."

"The Marquis must have archives concerning all his belongings and whatever else you do, my dear, try to be asked to go round The Castle. It really is one of the finest pieces of architecture in the whole of England."

Rosetta thought it would be a great mistake for her to push herself onto the Marquis, as he might guess she was not who she was pretending to be.

But this she could not say to her father.

Actually, she was very excited, first at the thought of staying at Waincliffe Hall, then meeting the man who was talked about continually, but seldom to his advantage.

She packed some of her prettiest clothes to wear in case none of Dolina's, which Lord Waincliffe had kindly suggested she might wear, fitted her.

She was only worried that her best evening gown, although attractive enough, would appear out of date.

She so seldom went out in the evening. Their local friends, if they had a party, usually asked her to luncheon, so she fancied that living quietly in the country, the clothes she thought of as her finest would be unfashionable.

'There is nothing I can do about it,' she told her reflection in the mirror.

So she began to wonder if Lord Waincliffe's sister, Dolina, arranged her hair differently to hers, but then she laughed, as it was highly unlikely that the Marquis would take any notice of her as a person.

What she had to do was to make him aware of how much a Racecourse was needed in the County.

And if they were talking about horses she was not afraid of appearing ignorant.

She had loved horses ever since she was a child and her father could not afford to provide her with more than two to ride.

The Master of Foxhounds, however, who was an old friend, often mounted her, especially when he had an obstreperous horse that no other lady in the County would ride.

"You are so kind to me," Rosetta had said to the Master after she had had a ride with him only a week ago and he had replied,

"When I see a horse like the one you have been riding today, I know that no one could handle it better than you. And I have come to the conclusion that women are either born good riders or else they are never completely at their ease in the saddle."

Rosetta had a way with horses that had fascinated quite a number of members of the Hunt and they invariably consulted her when they had a horse considered by others to be unrideable.

Her father had confided in her recently,

"I am so sorry, my dearest, that we cannot afford better bred horses, but the doctor's bills have been so large this year and I do feel ashamed of using up so much of our money on what appears to be a hopeless cause."

"I know that it's really maddening for you being so blind, Papa, but you are healthy in all other ways and you are not to talk like that until you have to walk on crutches."

"I hope to goodness that never happens to me!"

When she told him that she was going to The Hall, he had said,

"Be sure you take a good look at the stables and tell me what the horses are like. When I remember that I have ridden the most extraordinary animals in many parts of the world, I only wish I could now mount a really fine horse and ride it until we are both exhausted,"

He spoke with a yearning note in his voice, which made Rosetta feel sad, but so he would worry too much, she merely said,

"I promise, Papa, I will look at the horses and tell you all about them when I come back home – and I will not forget to ask the Marquis about the picture."

The carriage came for her from Waincliffe Hall.

After giving her aunt her last instructions as to how to make her father comfortable, she climbed into it.

She felt this was all very exciting.

It must, she mused, be at least eight years since she was last at Waincliffe Hall and she had only been eleven.

Her mother had taken her one day when her father was away and she had thought it very touching that Lord Waincliffe had been so very attentive to her mother and so delighted to welcome her as his guest.

Rosetta had been taken around the house by the butler, because her mother and Lord Waincliffe wanted to discuss some subjects they claimed she would find boring.

She had been thrilled with everything she had seen and before she left, Lord Waincliffe had given her several beautiful presents.

She had opened them feverishly as soon as she had climbed into the carriage.

There was a necklace of what she thought must be beads and it turned out to be of small pearls and so suitable for a young girl to wear.

And there had been a number of expensive books with pretty illustrations and these she had devoured.

Although she was really too old for it, there was an attractive doll and her mother said it must have cost a lot of money in a London shop.

It all came back to her now and how enchanting it had all been and how enormous The Hall had seemed.

'This is an adventure,' she now told herself, 'but, if I don't succeed in my task, they will never ask me again.'

It was only a short distance along the road from her house to the drive.

The gates looked impressive, but unfortunately they needed painting and repairing and the gilt had been washed away by the rain.

The drive was exactly as a drive should be, except that the boughs and leaves that had fallen from the trees in the winter were still lying on the ground.

Then she saw The Hall itself in the distance, rosy-pink in the evening sun with its windows glittering.

She felt that it was undoubtedly one of the most beautiful houses she could imagine and she was doubtful if even The Castle could be as impressive.

Gordon and Henry were waiting for her in the hall.

"You have come! You have come!" Henry cried. "And you look absolutely marvellous and exactly as we want you to be."

Rosetta knew he was really saying that she looked like his sister.

She merely smiled as Gordon shook her hand.

"I am more grateful to you than I can possibly say," he said. "Come along and let me show you the plans for the Racecourse. I want you to know everything about it before our visitor arrives."

"I thought you would," replied Rosetta. "I looked up some Racecourses that were illustrated in Papa's books. But I feel sure that your Racecourse will be different and more up-to-date than anything designed years ago."

"I hope so. Henry and I have been to most of the best Racecourses in the South of England and we want to improve on everything we have seen."

They took Rosetta into the study. As soon as the door was closed, Gordon said,

"Now, we must get into the habit of calling you 'Dolina' and not hesitating over the name as one is inclined to do if one thinks about it before saying it."

Rosetta laughed.

"I was just thinking that myself and I am honoured to have your sister's name. I have been told so often how beautiful and delightful she is."

"And so are *you*," added Gordon. "It is something you should not hide."

"I have no wish to, but there has been no one to impress with my beauty except my dogs!"

The two brothers chuckled and then they took her across the room to see the plans for the Racecourse.

"I think they are all marvellous," enthused Rosetta after having a good look at them.

Then rather shyly, she suggested two or three points that she thought could be improvements.

The brothers agreed with her at once and then they quickly incorporated them on the plans. Henry was a much better draughtsman than his brother.

"Now I expect you would like to see your room," suggested Gordon. "I am afraid there will be no one to look after you. Mrs. Barnes, whose husband is our butler, has been our cook for over twenty years."

"How wonderful!" Rosetta exclaimed.

"As she has very little help in the kitchen, she will be spending all her time preparing for dinner tonight."

"What time do you expect the Marquis to arrive?" Rosetta asked.

Henry made a gesture with his hands.

"When it suits him. We are both terrified he may change his mind at the last moment if he receives a better invitation, but we hope he will arrive soon after tea."

Rosetta knew by the way he was speaking that he was seriously worried that the Marquis might cancel his engagement with them.

She thought that if he did so she would despise him more than she did already.

She had, of course, not told Lord Waincliffe that she had always disliked what she had heard of the Marquis and she was horrified that he had paid so little attention to the County where he lived.

That he was a good landlord she could not deny and he did not neglect his employees or his vast estate, but he completely ignored most of the residents in the County.

He often brought his friends down from London for large parties, but he made no effort to include any of his neighbours.

Because they were ignored, it was natural that they spoke scornfully of him and repeated the most scandalous tales about him whenever his name was mentioned.

In fact since Rosetta had grown up, she had thought of him rather like a villain in a novel.

"I cannot imagine why he interests you so much," she said to one of her friends who had been repeating some recent scandal about the Marquis, which she had already heard from several others in the County.

Her friend had laughed.

"I suppose because we have little else to excite us and the Marquis certainly does behave, as you must admit, like the bogeyman in a children's book!"

"I should have thought you would have made him a hero," Rosetta remarked laughingly.

"I am not so stupid as that," her friend had replied. "And there is no doubt at all that he behaves disgracefully. We can only hope he is punished for his wicked ways."

There was a spiteful note in her voice and Rosetta knew that it was because she had never been invited to the Marquis's Castle.

She could not help thinking it amusing that, while most of the County had nothing better to talk about, the Marquis was enjoying himself in London.

He clearly had no idea that he was the inexhaustible subject of criticism at almost every party she attended.

According to local gossip, the Marquis would come down on a Friday night with anything up to twenty guests, all as distinguished as himself.

If they wished to dance, there was always a superb orchestra to play for them – and again the locals were not asked to join in.

On some occasions the parties were even larger and there would be music, singers, actors and dancers from London to entertain them.

Once again, there were no outsiders to report if the performance was good or bad.

Rosetta was quite certain it was extremely good and she was sure that the reason why the local ladies were so catty about these parties was that the Marquis never invited them.

They were obviously only for the ladies he brought from London with whom, again according to local rumour, he was having passionate *affaires de coeur*.

"You would think," Rosetta had said to her father not once but several times, "nothing else happens around here except at The Castle!"

"You cannot blame the young Marquis for enjoying himself," her father had answered. "But he is now getting older and will have to produce an heir sooner or later."

"Perhaps he does not want to be married?"

"Whether he wants it or not, he cannot allow his family, which was first heard about soon after the reign of William the Conqueror, to die out."

"No, of course not, and what would we do if there were no Millbrooks at The Castle for us to talk about?"

Her father had laughed.

"You are quite right, Rosetta. It would be very dull without him. If he does nothing else, he keeps the local tongues wagging!"

When Rosetta was shown into Dolina's bedroom, she said a little hesitatingly,

"I am just afraid that your guest, when he sees me tonight, will not think I am smart enough to be your sister."

"Do you remember," said Gordon, "that I suggested you should wear one of Dolina's gowns? She has a mass of clothes here and I imagine that just as you look alike, you are about the same size."

"Perhaps your sister would not mind my borrowing something from her," Rosetta remarked a little nervously.

Gordon grinned.

"For one thing she need not know and for another, as she has let us down, the very least she can do is to be generous to the very kind lady who has taken over her part on the stage."

"I only hope I am experienced enough to enthral the audience!"

"To do so, you must be properly dressed for the part," Gordon replied firmly. "Choose from her wardrobe a dress that you think will be the most becoming."

Dolina had taken the prettiest furniture from other rooms to decorate hers – there were several mirrors with beautiful frames covered with china cupids and flowers.

There were also very elaborate curtains on her bed and her dressing table was covered with every sort of face-creams and beautifiers.

When Gordon opened the wardrobe doors, Rosetta could only gasp.

She had never seen such a collection of beautiful and fashionable gowns and she was sure that all of them had cost a great deal of money and they were certainly unobtainable anywhere except in Bond Street.

Considering how poor she knew Lord Waincliffe and his brother were, she could not understand how their sister could own such lovely and expensive garments.

Guessing her thoughts, Gordon reminded her.

"My sister is very fortunate in her rich Godmother, who presented her at Court. She also gave her all these magnificent dresses."

He paused for a moment before he added,

"I cannot think there will be any use for them down here, unless, of course, you are so tactful and clever with the Marquis that she is invited to The Castle."

"I will do my best and I would love to borrow some of these glorious gowns."

"Make your choice," Gordon invited her, "and if I know anything of my sister, they will all be replaced as soon as she goes back to London!"

It was a temptation Rosetta could not resist.

She then chose one of the most glamorous evening gowns she had ever seen and knew it would become her better than any dress she had ever worn.

Gordon left her as he wanted to make quite certain that everything was perfect in the room where the Marquis was to sleep.

He and Henry had asked him if he would stay the night as they had so much to discuss and they had been astonished when he actually said he would do so.

They had quite expected him to leave after dinner to drive back to The Castle, as it was not very far away.

"If you ask me," Henry had muttered when Gordon exclaimed with delight at the Marquis's acceptance, "it's because he wants to see if we are really fit enough to be his partners in anything as demanding as a Racecourse."

Gordon had laughed.

"I didn't think of that, but I expect you are right. I only hope the dinner is edible and his bed does not collapse under him for lack of repair!"

Henry had chuckled, but he knew that beneath his joking Gordon was very nervous that the Marquis would think they were not grand or rich enough to be his partners.

Having selected a gown to wear at dinner, Rosetta took some time in choosing what she would wear now so that she looked her best when the Marquis arrived.

If he was on time, that would be not long after six o'clock.

Finally she chose an afternoon dress which was, she thought, grand enough to be worn at Marlborough House. It was designed to frame a woman's beauty and make her look extremely striking.

She took both gowns to her room and then changed into the stunning afternoon dress.

It was the blue of her eyes and to her relief it fitted her exactly as it must have fitted its rightful owner.

When she now looked at herself in the mirror, she thought that never before had she realised just how good a figure she had or how small her waist was.

The blue of the gown accentuated the clear pink and white beauty of her skin and, as she gazed at herself again in the mirror, she wished her father's eyes were good enough for him to see her now.

She took yet another look and hoped that she was really like the girl she was now impersonating, as after all Dolina had been acclaimed as one of the great beauties of Mayfair.

'If I let them down they, will never forgive me,' Rosetta ruminated.

If she did, it would be a humiliation that would haunt her for the rest of her life.

Then, because it was something she always did, she prayed that she would be a big success and that the two brothers who had been so kind to her would achieve what they wanted – their Racecourse.

It was well after six o'clock when Rosetta, after a last look at herself in the mirror, walked slowly down the stairs.

She peeped in at the drawing room as she passed it and at two other rooms she thought very impressive but obviously not used.

However, she told herself that she must not waste time and that she would take another look at the plans of the Racecourse, as it would be fatal to make any mistakes if the Marquis questioned her about it.

As she expected, she found the two brothers in the study.

They rose when she came in through the door.

For a moment, they just stared at her.

Then Gordon cried out,

"You look smashing, marvellous and so beautiful!"

"I swear, and I am not just being polite," Henry came in, "that you are much lovelier than Dolina."

"I would like to think that's true," Rosetta smiled. "But I am glad you are pleased with me, although actually you are congratulating your sister's dress-maker rather than me."

"We are just saying that you look exactly as we wanted you to look," added Gordon. "To put you at ease, I swear, if I did not know who you were, I would think you were my sister, Dolina."

"That is what I want you to say," smiled Rosetta. "Now, let me look again at the plans so that I know them as I should do if I had been with you talking about nothing else for months."

Henry laughed.

"That is true enough. It has been hovering over us like a dark cloud. If we don't win tonight, I think we will just give up hope and leave England for the Colonies!"

He was only joking and Rosetta giggled,

"You will very likely find the same problem there. What we all need, if we are honest, is *money*."

"That is indeed very true," said Gordon. "It seems extraordinary, when you read about my grandfather and my great-grandfather, to learn they were all so rich. Yet when my father died there was practically nothing left at all – "

"Except this lovely house," Rosetta interrupted.

"A lovely house that is falling down. I learnt only this afternoon from Barnes that the ceiling in one of the second floor bedrooms collapsed last night."

"Oh, not another!" Henry exclaimed.

"I am afraid so and Barnes said we will be lucky if in the next few months there are not two more."

"Don't talk about such things at present," Rosetta said. "I believe if you want something badly enough, like the Racecourse, you have to be sure in yourself that you will obtain it."

Gordon stared at her before responding,

"You are quite right. If you start a race on a horse feeling doubtful if you will win, you don't have a chance."

"I think the same applies to other things. So we must now tell ourselves that we are going to persuade the Marquis that the Racecourse is necessary and that it will be a feather in his cap as well as ours if it becomes a reality."

"Yes, that is what we will do," Henry said quickly.

"Indeed we will," Gordon agreed. "You are quite right, Rosetta, and we will both rely on you to make the Marquis fully aware of the benefits he will receive from this venture."

"What you must realise, is that it will make him very popular in the County. While, as it is, he is quite the most unpopular man there has ever been."

"I would never have thought of that," Gordon said. "It is certainly a point you might suggest to him tactfully."

"Very tactfully – or he may take umbrage," Rosetta smiled. "But actually it's true, because he keeps his Castle only for his London friends and has no interest in anything locally – and so everybody hates him."

"I suppose it's a form of jealousy."

"Of course it is," Rosetta agreed. "He has so much and the average local has very little in comparison. Even the Lord Lieutenant the other day said he was hard-up and I always thought he was a very rich man."

"He was only saying that to make you sympathise with him. He owns over a dozen of the finest horses and though his house is not so impressive, it's very comfortable and he drinks the best champagne every night!"

"That's a sure sign that he's not only well off, but perhaps, as he is complaining he does not have more, he is also a miser."

"Now you are making a story out of it," Gordon asserted. "There is no doubt that if you wrote one, it would be a best seller! The whole plot would centre around the Marquis."

"That is just what I thought when I was dressing. I was wondering whether I should make him the hero or the villain. I suppose to make a really good tale of it, he would repent of his sins and become the hero!"

"That just never happens in real life," Henry said scornfully. "And if you ask me, the one person who enjoys being the villain is the Marquis!"

Even as he spoke, the door opened.

"There be no sign of his Lordship as yet," Barnes reported, "so shall I take away the tea?"

"Yes, take it away, Barnes," Gordon sighed.

As he spoke, he walked towards the plans for the Racecourse.

CHAPTER THREE

The Marquis stirred and then realised he had been asleep.

As he opened his eyes, something soft and gentle against his shoulder murmured,

"Oh, Euan darling, if only we could always be like this, how wonderful life would be!"

He had heard women say those same words many times and quite suddenly and for no particular reason, it irritated him.

He did not answer and an arm went round his neck.

It was only with the greatest difficulty he did not fight it off.

He did not really understand it himself, but this had happened to him before.

Quite unexpectedly, he was tired of the liaison that had seemed so exciting and now he wanted only to be free.

'*Free*' was indeed perhaps the right word.

Ever since he had left Eton, there had been women pursuing him and trying to catch him.

The beautiful woman he had taken to bed tonight had been, when he had first pursued her, someone he felt was strangely unique.

She had been different from all the others on whom he had bestowed his favours, but now he was aware that the excitement and thrill had begun to fade a week ago.

Suddenly the curtain came down as if on a stage drama and then all he desired was to be alone with himself.

With some difficulty, because he must behave like a gentleman, he managed to blurt out,

"It's now late, Hermione, and I must go home."

She gave a shriek of horror.

"But, darling, it's nowhere near dawn. We might have to wait for a long time before we can have another wonderful night like this together."

The Marquis thought that was a relief at any rate!

Yet naturally he did not say so.

He merely took her arms gently from around his neck and pressed her back against the lace-edged pillow.

"You are very lovely," he sighed, "but like me, you need your beauty sleep."

"Not if I can be with you, Euan."

Her voice was low and seductive as she went on,

"I love and adore you. Oh, Euan, you are really so wonderful. No one has ever had a finer lover. How can I ever let you go?"

The Marquis thought she was once again trying to catch him in a trap – to make him hers when all he wanted at this very moment was sleep!

It took him another ten minutes before at last he managed to climb out of bed and start to dress.

Hermione protested again as he did so.

"How can you leave me when I need you so much? Tonight we have not had to worry that Gerald might return. He is on his way to Doncaster and will be away for three days and three *nights*."

The Marquis did not answer and she continued,

"We can be together tomorrow, and after luncheon, which I know you are having with the Beauforts, as I am, we can return here. Oh, Euan, it will be marvellous!"

The Marquis pressed his lips together.

He had found the letter he had received from Lord Waincliffe more interesting than the luncheon party he had accepted.

But he thought, as he was planning what he would do, the luncheon would be dull affair.

As he was silent, Hermione gave a little scream.

"You are not thinking of avoiding the Beaufort's party?" she asked. "The Prince of Wales is certain to be there and he always likes talking to you."

The Marquis knew this to be true.

If there was one person he had no wish to offend, it was the Prince of Wales and he always enjoyed himself at Marlborough House more than anywhere else.

The Prince was quickly bored and so he gathered around him the most interesting and intelligent men and, of course, without question the most beautiful women.

Then the Marquis remembered that he was not after all going to the Beaufort's party as he was having luncheon with the Prince of Wales at Marlborough House.

It would, he thought, be a mistake to tell Hermione.

"Yes, indeed," he said aloud, "I will see you at the Beauforts, but I am afraid I have to leave for the country as soon as luncheon is over."

"Leave for the country!" Hermione almost shrieked as she sat bolt upright up in bed. "How can you *possibly* go to the country when we can be together?"

He did not answer and she rambled on,

"I have been counting on our dining here tomorrow night. In fact, I have refused at least three invitations in order to be with you.

"Then you must forgive me, but I have to go home. There are difficulties only I can solve."

"How could that mean more to you than I do?" she asked angrily.

Because there was a deep reproach in her voice, the Marquis responded,

"No one, as you know, matters more than you. But sadly I have my responsibilities and this is one of them."

She threw herself back against the pillows, making a cry of agony.

"I have so looked forward to this. Oh, Euan, how can you be so unkind to me when I love you – I love you!"

As she repeated the words, her voice rose.

The Marquis reflected that what he disliked more than anything else was hysterical women.

He might have guessed before now that, if things did not go exactly as she herself desired, Hermione would become overemotional.

"You must not upset yourself," he told her, as he buttoned up his waistcoat. "You know I would hate you to be unhappy."

"I am only happy when I am with you. I love you, I worship you, Euan. If you leave me, I will kill myself. I cannot face life without you!"

The Marquis had heard all this before – yet so far no one had actually committed suicide on his behalf.

Where the great beauties were concerned, they had soon replaced him with another man.

He looked in the mirror and saw by the light of the candle by the bed that he was looking as neat and as smart as when he had arrived.

He turned round and moved towards the bed where Hermione was lying, looking like the Goddess of Love.

Her figure was superb and indeed a number of men had compared her with Venus and she had no doubt that she was, in every man's eyes, the perfect woman they all longed to find.

Her dark hair was falling over her shoulders and her arms were outstretched in a manner her lovers had always found irresistible.

She could not believe that the Marquis would be able to leave her.

"Kiss me, Euan," she cooed very softly. "Let me tell you just how handsome you are and how my heart is beating at your touch."

Her voice was deep and seductive and the Marquis again thought that he had heard all this many times before.

He knew quite well that if he kissed her, she would pull him back down onto the bed.

Then it would be even more difficult than it was already for him to escape.

"You are so very lovely, Hermione," he said, going towards the door, "I can only thank you for giving me such a rapturous and sublime evening."

"Kiss me, Euan," she begged. "Kiss me."

She lifted herself up so that he could see the beauty of her body.

But the door was open and he was already halfway through it.

"Sleep well, Hermione," he called, "so that you will look even more beautiful at luncheon tomorrow."

As she gave a little cry of protest, he was gone.

She heard him walking along the passage that led to the top of the stairs and for a moment she could not believe that he had not listened to her.

He had left her when she still wanted him.

Then, as she realised he had really gone and that she was alone, she struck at the pillows in sheer rage with her clenched fists.

She had been so certain he was completely hers.

When Gerald had gone to the races at Doncaster, she had known this was the opportunity they had both been waiting for.

So she could hardly believe that the Marquis was telling her the truth, when he had declared that he would be leaving London tomorrow to go to the country.

How could he possibly leave her?

For the first time in nearly two weeks they had been able to make love without being afraid. There had always been the chance that the door would open and her husband would walk in.

It had been, Hermione believed, one of the great occasions in her life.

She had captured the Marquis of Millbrook!

Of course she had met him at many different parties and he had always been taken up with some woman or else he had left early because he was very obviously bored.

She had known that she had captured his attention when they had met at Marlborough House four weeks ago.

It had been a triumph for her, as the competition was intense.

The Prince of Wales had chosen to invite all the most outstanding beauties to a special party with only his most special gentlemen friends.

Hermione had admired the Marquis for a long time and had tried by every means in her repertoire to attract his attention.

He had always been polite and courteous whenever they met, but he had not shown any desire to see her again.

The invitations she had sent to him on behalf of her husband and herself were always refused. He wrote that it was regrettable that he was already engaged and had signed the letters himself. She was sure that they had been written by his secretary and he had merely added his signature.

Then, when she least expected it, he had sat next to her at a dinner party at Marlborough House.

Before the evening was over, she had realised her dreams had come true.

They had met subsequently several times and she had become more and more infatuated by him, but it was, however, impossible for them to make love, because her husband was always with her.

Besides, he harboured what she considered to be a quite unreasonable dislike of the Marquis.

"He is far too pleased with himself for one thing," Gerald pronounced, "and I find his love affairs exceedingly tedious."

"I expect you are jealous," Hermione had retorted, "because the Marquis is such a success with women. The Duchess of Devonshire was saying only the other week, he was undoubtedly the most handsome man in Mayfair and his love affairs would fill at least three books!"

"It's the sort of thing women would think," Gerald had replied sourly. "Let me make it clear, I have no wish to entertain that Marquis in my house."

He walked out of the room as he spoke to her and slammed the door behind him.

She knew it was because he was jealous and he had every reason to be so, as she was so beautiful she had been pursued by almost every man in the *Beau Monde* since she married.

But whatever Gerald might think or do to prevent it, she was determined that the Marquis should be hers.

She was certain that she would hold him as no other woman had ever been able to do.

"I cannot think why he left me," one of her friends had sobbed. "I loved him with all my heart, but suddenly for no reason I could understand, he went away."

She cried again before adding,

"The next thing I knew he was with another woman and one I have always hated, who naturally was delighted to be able to crow over me because I had lost him."

Hermione had not felt particularly sorry for her.

But now she was lying alone in her exotic bedroom, which was scented with flowers and French perfume.

She felt a horror that the Marquis might have left her for ever.

*

Walking home, because their houses were near to each other, the Marquis felt the cool night air a relief.

He had escaped and for once it was without tears from another trap that had been set to catch him.

It was absurd, he told himself.

Yet he had always felt, when a woman surrendered herself to him, that it was really he who had surrendered his freedom, which was so precious to him.

He thought somewhat cynically that he knew every twist and turn of the game and every word they would utter to keep him their prisoner and prevent him from slipping out of their grasp.

Of course, he found women attractive.

Of course, he was well aware that other men were envious of him because he attracted women so easily.

But at the same time there was something he did not understand.

Why, when a lovely woman twined her arms round him and told him passionately of her love, should he want to escape?

It was a strange feeling he could not control and it prevented him from surrendering himself as completely as the woman surrendered herself to him.

He loved a woman for her beauty.

He loved the way she would flirt with him as soon as they met, the look in her eyes that told him only too clearly that she wanted him to make love to her.

Sometimes, when they had particularly possessive husbands, it was impossible and then he thought he would be missing something he would have greatly enjoyed.

But on most occasions they would surrender far too quickly.

In many cases, as with Hermione, they themselves organised the love affair.

This would mean that he did little to bring the affair to a climax – they would manipulate him into it rather than him forcing himself upon them.

He knew as he walked back down the empty and silent street that if he was honest he did not even want to see Hermione again.

She was beautiful and had responded to him in a way that had ignited the fire in him.

But that was all.

'What more do I want?' he asked himself, as he turned into Park Lane.

He did not know the answer to this question now any better than he had before, he only knew that something vital was missing, something that affected his mind rather than his body.

A sleepy night-footman let him into his large and grand house and he handed the man his hat and cane.

"Goodnight, James."

"Goodnight, my Lord."

The Marquis then walked up the stairs and along the corridor to his own room, which was as was large and magnificent as the rest of his London house.

Everything had been left ready for him, so he only had to undress himself and climb into bed.

He deliberately did not keep his valet up as other men did and anyway he had no wish to speak to anyone when he was tired.

He also disliked giving his servants anything to talk about where his love affairs were concerned.

He was quite certain that below stairs they would speculate as to who was his latest conquest and compare the time he came home at night with other evenings when they knew he was out with a particularly famous beauty.

He was still asking himself just why he no longer wished to stay with Hermione, as he drew back the curtains and opened the window wider.

He was looking out over the trees in Hyde Park and thought that if it had not been closed for the night he would have liked to walk down to the Serpentine.

Then he told himself there was a long day in front of him tomorrow and so the sooner he went to sleep the better.

Yet, when he finally climbed into bed, he found himself ruminating again that yet another of his love affairs had come to an end.

He was still not at all certain why.

It was the sort of question he had asked himself a dozen times and had never found an answer.

Hermione was indeed beautiful – in fact, her beauty had been acclaimed in every magazine and she actually rivalled the Jersey Lily in the number of people who stood on chairs in Hyde Park to see her drive past.

She was witty and well educated and she listened more attentively to him than other women managed to do.

Then why, why, he asked himself when she had told him they could be together for another two nights, had he not wished to be with her?

If the truth be told he had actually, when dressing that evening, thought that perhaps he would not go to the country after all tomorrow.

He felt certain that Lord Waincliffe merely had something boring to discuss with him about their adjoining estates – the poaching might be more aggressive than his gamekeepers had bothered to tell him or maybe there were too many foxes.

The burning fire within himself and Hermione had risen higher and higher.

They had both been consumed by it.

Yet he had known at the back of his mind that it was not what he sought, but he was unable to tell himself exactly what that was.

He only knew that, as she expressed her love and delight in him, what he murmured in response was no more than automatic.

He had said it so often and, even as the words left his lips, he knew that they were not the truth.

He wanted something else, something intangible to which he could not put a name.

He was only too well aware that his reputation was appalling and he was teased at the Club by those who knew him well. It did not worry him and he was quite prepared to laugh at himself.

He was especially amused when mothers with their beautiful daughters hurried them out of his sight, but he had never been interested in *debutantes*. He realised only too well that, if he did, he would then be hurried up the aisle immediately by her ambitious parents.

If he attempted to protest, he would be confronted by the traditional rules of the Social world.

If a young virgin's character was put at risk, the only possible reparation for any gentleman was to offer her a wedding ring.

The Marquis had therefore been very careful and so all his *affaires-de-coeur* were with married women whose husbands were either complacent or had business or their own entertainment elsewhere.

Even so, with a long trail of broken hearts behind him, he was still seeking the unseekable.

'What *do* I want?' he asked himself again as he gazed out of the window. 'What is missing?'

He could not give himself an answer to any of his questions and it annoyed him that he was so stupid, as he pulled the curtain to.

Blowing out the candle, he climbed into bed.

Tomorrow he would go to the country.

And before he left, he would send Hermione a huge basket of orchids and a letter thanking her for a delightful and unforgettable evening.

He would then inevitably receive a long stream of letters from her, each of them complaining more violently than the last that he had not been to see her and that she had waited for him in vain.

He did not like to think how many such letters he had received on exactly the same theme and to which he had made no reply.

The letters had always asked him finally before the correspondence ceased why he no longer wanted them.

Why he refused their love? In fact, to put it plainly, why he had not been eager to be in bed with them again?

The truth was that he had no valid answer and he could not reason it out even to himself.

But just as the curtain had fallen on a number of other beautiful women, he knew he had no wish to even see Hermione again.

Why? Why?

The words seemed to hang above him in the quiet darkness.

When at last he fell asleep, it was to dream that he was climbing up a high mountain.

When eventually he managed to reach the top, there was nothing there – the mountain itself did not exist!

*

He woke with a start when his valet called him at eight o'clock sharp and drew back the curtains.

The Marquis recalled what had happened last night.

How he had left Hermione much earlier than she expected and in consequence he had had an exceptionally long night's sleep.

Quite suddenly, it occurred to him that it would be a joy and a delight to be in the country.

He would be alone at The Castle.

Yet, he would have to attend the luncheon first at Marlborough House – that went without saying.

But he was determined to leave at a reasonable hour as the journey would take him at least four hours.

And then he remembered he had promised Lord Waincliffe to stay the night with him.

Perhaps he had been a fool to agree to do so, as he would have been much more content in his Castle with all his treasures around him.

Then he told himself that, even if Waincliffe was a bore, it would be far better than being alone at home and asking himself the same questions over and over again.

'Why do I feel like this?' he asked himself. 'Why does this happen to me? Why can I not be like other men and be content with a beautiful woman?"

The questions were back and haunting him.

He rode out most mornings in Rotten Row simply for exercise, as he was afraid that too much good food and drink would ruin his splendid figure.

As he expected, the smart set were there cracking jokes with him if they were riding or waving pretty gloved hands from open carriages.

There were a number of women looking at him with questioning eyes and he reckoned that they were just as beautiful as when he had last seen them – perhaps even *more* beautiful than when he had last made love to them.

There were also some who turned their heads away when he raised his hat to them. It was either because they hated him for leaving them or if they were older, because they were shocked at his increasingly poor reputation.

He never stayed long in Rotten Row – instead he galloped round the back of the Park and then home to his own Mews.

There were a dozen letters waiting for him when he finished breakfast and he gave his secretary orders to send Hermione an elaborate arrangement of orchids.

His secretary had been with him a long time.

"I think, my Lord," he began earnestly, "they are grossly overcharging us at that shop in Bond Street. I am told there's a new man in Shepherd's Market who sells the same flowers at half the price."

The Marquis shrugged his shoulders.

"I will leave it to you, Walters, but there is no need to economise on such trivial things."

He paused before he continued,

"I hear that there are some exceptionally fine horses coming up at Tattersall's next week and I am determined if possible to purchase the best of them."

His secretary smiled.

"If you buy many more, my Lord, you will have to build some more stables for them at The Castle."

"I did not think of that, but I will have a look to see if they are overcrowded when I am there tomorrow."

"Are you staying the night, my Lord, at Waincliffe Hall? Is there anything in particular Your Lordship wishes to take with you?"

"Nothing I can think of and I cannot imagine why they would want to see me, unless it is to complain about poaching in our woods."

"I have heard," said Mr. Walters, "that there are some excellent pictures at Waincliffe Hall. His Lordship also has an exceptional collection of snuffboxes."

"That's sounds unusual and so I will look forward to seeing them."

"I think they were all collected during the French Revolution by one of his ancestors," Mr. Walters added, "and their pictures have been handed down for centuries. Lord Waincliffe's great-grandfather was really determined to acquire a picture gallery to rival your Lordship's."

"And did he succeed?"

"I have been told he was not far off it."

The Marquis was interested.

He had thought after promising to stay the night at Waincliffe Hall that he had made a mistake and however late after dinner, he should have insisted on going home.

Now he thought it would be interesting to see the Waincliffe picture gallery.

Could Lord Waincliffe's really rival his own? He had to admit he had been rather lazy about it and had not added either to his picture gallery or to his other treasures for at least four years.

'Too many women and nothing to show for it,' he surmised.

Then he became annoyed at being so cynical about himself, as he had seldom been before in his life.

'It would be irritating,' he reflected, 'if Waincliffe could boast that he has a better collection of anything than I have at The Castle.'

His letters, as there were so many of them, took longer than he expected and he had to assure Mr. Walters that he would finish them off after he had returned from Marlborough House to pick up his luggage.

"I don't want to seem a nuisance, my Lord," Mr. Walters said, "but you started a letter last week to the Duke of Devonshire and you have not yet finished it."

"If I remember he was asking me a lot of questions to which I had no answer, but put it out for me and I will finish it before I leave."

"Thank you, my Lord. I dislike bothering you, but it's a mistake to get behind with all this correspondence."

"You are right to bully me, Walters, and I promise I will do what is needed before I leave."

He arrived at Marlborough House just in time not to annoy his host.

It was well known that the Prince of Wales was always on time and if he was kept waiting, he tapped his fingers impatiently on the table or whatever was near him and was furious with the culprit when he did appear.

The Marquis scraped in by the skin of his teeth and when the Prince received him, he commented,

"I was beginning to think you had forgotten me, Euan."

"I would never do that, Sire," the Marquis replied. "But I have some interesting news to tell you when I have the opportunity."

He had no idea what this was, but he knew that this promise would bring a light into the Prince's eyes.

If there was one thing His Royal Highness enjoyed, it was being told a secret before anyone else knew it or being given some information he hitherto had not known.

It did not matter what it was. He just wanted to be the first.

When they went into luncheon, the Marquis found that he was sitting next to a very pretty lady.

He had admired her at other parties, but they had not previously met and when he asked her why this was, she replied that she had been abroad.

"In fact I have been to India with my father who is *aide-de-camp* to the Viceroy. I am only back in England with him because he has been very ill and is only at this moment off the danger list."

"I wondered why I had never met you before," the Marquis murmured. "But now I am gratified to do so."

She smiled at him and he knew without her saying so that she found him even more attractive than she had been told he would be.

"Now at last we have met," he added, "but what are we going to do about it."

"What do you want to do?" she enquired.

There was an expression in her eyes that he knew only too well.

"I will tell you about it in detail later on, but just in case our host has prior claim on your attention, will you give me the address where you are staying in London so that I may be in touch with you?"

He realised as he spoke that she was delighted at his question.

A few minutes later, he felt her slip a card into his pocket whilst he was speaking to the guest on his left.

When luncheon was over and a number of guests started to leave, including the lovely lady on his right, the Marquis was unable to accompany her.

The Prince of Wales said he particularly wanted to speak to him.

As he said goodbye to her, he felt that her fingers trembled in his and he recognised that he had made another conquest.

"I have to go to the country," he said in a low voice which no one else could hear, "but I will be in touch with you when I return."

"That will be very exciting for me," she replied, "and I will look forward to it."

He thought, as he looked at her again, that she was extremely pretty and he liked the softness of her voice.

"You will not forget?" she simpered, as she turned towards the door.

"You can be sure I will not," the Marquis answered.

The Prince of Wales then took him into his private sitting room.

"What do you think of the delightful creature I put next to you at luncheon?" he asked.

"Exactly what Your Royal Highness expected me to think!"

The Prince of Wales laughed.

"She is indeed very lovely and I thought you would appreciate her more than anyone else."

"I could never doubt you on a matter of taste, Sire," the Marquis replied.

"And what about Hermione?" he questioned before the Marquis could speak again. "I was told that she is very much in love with you."

The Marquis did not answer and after a moment the Prince of Wales exclaimed,

"It cannot be over! Not as quickly as *that*!"

"I am afraid so, Sire."

"Well all I can say, Euan," the Prince smiled, "is, if you gobble up a particularly good meal too quickly, you end up with indigestion!"

The Marquis laughed.

"That is one way of putting it, Sire. But I find it difficult to move slowly in anything."

"We are all aware of that, Euan!"

"Now do tell me about the horses you intend to buy that belonged to poor Christopher. I have heard they are coming up at Tattersall's next week."

They talked on about horses until the Marquis was aware he was already late in leaving London.

He made his apologies to the Prince of Wales and left, promising to come to Marlborough House as soon as he returned from the country.

Mr. Walters was waiting for him at the house in Park Lane and the Marquis signed a dozen letters while his luggage was being put into his superb phaeton.

He set out nearly an hour later than he intended, but he recognised he had the right team to make up the time.

They were beautifully matched and he had bought them from their previous owner, who had almost wept in sorrow when he had to part with them.

"It was only because I have been fool enough to lose a lot of money at White's," he said, "that I am offering you this team. I know that no one will appreciate them more than you."

"I am exceedingly grateful to you," the Marquis said. "They are without exception the best looking horses I have seen for a long time and I will enjoy driving them."

"I enjoyed them myself," the owner told him, "but I am almost broke and you would be the one person who would appreciate them and who would not beat me down from the price they are worth."

The Marquis knew he was being asked, because he was rich, to pay more than anyone else would, but because he was sorry for him and keen to have the horses, he had paid without querying the cost.

Now, as he set out from Park Lane, he knew that the price he had paid for the team had not been too much.

His valet was sitting beside him and his groom was in the seat at the back.

Once they were out in the country and London was behind them, the Marquis gave his horses their heads and they were even better than he anticipated.

When they arrived at the village at the bottom of the drive to Waincliffe Hall, he knew he was only an hour late and, if he had been driving his other horses, he would undoubtedly have taken another hour.

"I only hope," he said, as they turned in at the rather dilapidated gates, "that they have plenty of comfortable accommodation for this team, which deserves, even more than we do, a good night's rest."

His valet laughed.

"That be true, my Lord, but I've been clenchin' me teeth once or twice in case we had an accident."

"You should trust me, David. In the ten years you have been my valet, we have not had a crash yet."

"Cross your fingers, my Lord, and don't question your luck!"

"As far as I am concerned, this is the best team I have ever owned and I am very proud of them."

David did not reply as they drew up at the front door.

The Marquis had no idea that his servants were heaving a deep sigh of relief that they had actually arrived.

CHAPTER FOUR

Gordon walked forward holding out his hand.

"I am delighted to greet you, my Lord," he said. "I was afraid you had either forgotten us or had been held up on the way."

"The latter is my excuse," responded the Marquis. "Actually it was His Royal Highness who held me up, so I feel sure you will forgive me."

"We are so delighted that you have arrived safely. This is my brother Henry – and my sister Dolina."

Rosetta had been keeping in the background, but now she came forward and held out her hand.

"So we meet at last," the Marquis declared. "I have heard so much about you. You are exactly as I expected."

Rosetta smiled,

"We are so glad you have arrived. Did your horses break any record coming here?"

"As a matter of fact they did!"

It passed through the Marquis's mind that this was extraordinary.

No woman had ever before asked about his horses when he had started referring to her beauty.

"We have made it in only five minutes over four hours and I am sure that's better than you or I have done in the past."

"It certainly is," exclaimed Henry. "You must have superlative horses to achieve it."

"They are a new team to me and have turned out even better than I anticipated."

"Well, now you are here," said Gordon, "I am sure you would like to wash before we have dinner and please don't bother to change as it is quite an informal meal."

"I am glad to hear that and I would like to wash."

"But I feel sure that first," Henry suggested, "you would like a glass of champagne. It has been on ice for you and we did not dare touch it until you arrived."

"That was very abstemious of you and I promise not to drink the whole bottle myself!" the Marquis replied.

Gordon poured him out a glass of champagne.

He was hoping as he did so that Mrs. Barnes was not dishing up dinner as soon as their guest had arrived.

The Marquis drank a sip of champagne and then he proposed,

"As I am delaying your meal and you are doubtless hungry, I will take the champagne up with me, if I may, while you show me the way upstairs."

"I will carry it for you," Gordon offered, taking it from him.

He led the way from the study and up the stairs.

He was aware, as he did so, that the Marquis was looking around him as if he was somewhat surprised at the pictures and the furniture.

Gordon could only hope that he did not look at the cracked ceilings or at the walls that, where they were not panelled, all needed replastering.

The Marquis, however, was apologising once again for being late.

"I don't know if you have ever been invited to Marlborough House," he said, "but if you have, you will recall that His Royal Highness always has something of import to say to you just when you are ready to leave."

Gordon laughed.

"I have heard the story."

"In fact," the Marquis continued, "some of my friends deliberately make a move to leave early, knowing that otherwise they will be late for their next appointment."

"Why do you think he does that?" Gordon asked because he was interested.

"His Royal Highness loves to have people round him and, when one party ends, he feels lost until he starts the next one."

They had by now reached the room chosen for the Marquis and it was very attractive.

The setting sun was coming in a rosy haze through the open windows.

The Marquis's valet already had taken his evening clothes out of his trunk and had them laid out on the bed.

"There is no need to hurry, my Lord. As we keep country hours, they are, I promise you, very expandable when we have friends from London."

"That is very kind of you and I promise I will not be any longer than necessary."

Leaving the Marquis's room, Gordon ran as quickly as he could down the stairs.

Barnes was waiting in the hall and Gordon blurted out breathlessly,

"His Lordship is going to change after all. Will you tell your wife it will be a quarter of an hour or perhaps longer before we can start dinner."

"Don't worry, my Lord," Barnes said soothingly. "I've been here long enough to appreciate that guests from

London always find the journey longer than they expects. I tells the Missus first thing this morning that your Lordship won't be eating until London time and that won't be till nigh on nine o'clock."

Gordon gave a sigh of relief.

"Barnes you are a genius. I thought dinner would be ruined and Mrs. Barnes in tears."

"Now don't you fuss, my Lord."

Barnes spoke to him in the same tranquil voice he had used when Gordon and Henry were small boys.

"Everything will turn out for the best and everyone in the kitchen, the garden and on the estate be praying that His Lordship'll be forthcoming."

"We can only hope and pray," Gordon agreed, as he turned to walk towards the study, thinking they would be lost without Barnes.

"At least he has come," Henry sighed with relief when Gordon entered the room.

"I told you not to worry. Anyone who comes from London finds it takes longer than they think. All we can say is – thank God he's arrived."

Henry turned towards Rosetta.

"What do you think of him? he asked. "I know you have never met him before."

"I have heard so much about him and in point of fact he looks exactly as I expected."

"He is certainly handsome," Gordon added, "and it's not surprising that women run after him."

"And *he* runs after *them*," Henry chimed in.

Rosetta did not comment.

She walked to the window and stood looking out at the sun, now sinking in the sky and throwing long shadows in front of the trees and the fountain.

She was not aware that the fountain had not worked for a long time, but Gordon insisted it must play when the Marquis arrived.

Rosetta thought it was all even more beautiful than she was prepared for.

Gordon then joined her at the window.

"I thought you would be pleased with the fountain," he said. "We had a terrible job to get it going, but it makes the garden look more attractive than it has for years."

"I do love a fountain," sighed Rosetta.

Then she noticed Gordon drumming his fingers on the windowsill.

"Don't be over-anxious," she said quietly. "That is always a mistake when something vital is at stake."

"How can I be anything else?" Gordon asked.

"You will just have to trust in fate and be confident, as it's such a good idea and so beneficial to a great number of people, that you will be successful."

Gordon smiled at her.

"That is exactly the right thing to say and of course you are right. It's stupid of me to be nervous and on edge."

"Exactly," Rosetta asserted. "If people know you are feeling like that and they often know instinctively, then they are inclined to be put off before you have driven home the importance of the idea you are promoting."

"Now, Rosetta, you are talking as if you are my grandmother. I cannot think how you can be so wise and at the same time so beautiful."

"I take after my mother who was both!"

Then to his surprise, she turned and walked back towards Henry, who was standing in front of the fireplace and, she realised, watching the door.

Gordon was staring at Rosetta and he thought that she was undoubtedly the loveliest girl he had ever seen in his whole life.

Although it seemed incredible, she was even more beautiful than his sister and yet the resemblance was still striking.

Although he did not want to think about it, he kept remembering the tale he had heard.

His father, twenty odd years ago, had been very attentive to Mrs. Stourton when her husband was away and she was alone. He was either at the University or taking his students on special expeditions round the world.

Gordon had, although he had not said anything to Henry, been completely astonished when Rosetta told them her Christian name.

It had definitely been one of his father's favourite names and he had actually called his special mare Rosetta as well as a boat he had owned at one time.

Whether what was frequently suspected about his father's relationship with Mrs. Stourton was true or not, Gordon did not want to think about it at this moment.

He therefore turned round to watch the fountain.

As it threw its water high up into the air, he thought it accurately symbolised all that he and Henry were doing with their ambition over the Racecourse.

To them it was an exciting and irresistible venture and yet it might seem very different to the Marquis.

In just fifteen minutes, rather sooner than Gordon reckoned, the Marquis reappeared.

He was now looking even more handsome in his evening clothes.

When he entered the study, Gordon could not help giving a shout of joy.

"You have broken another record, my Lord. No one has ever managed to change so quickly and we ought to award you a special prize!"

The Marquis smiled.

"I have learnt to be quick in everything I do," he said, "and especially in making up my mind."

Henry had brought another glass of champagne and he accepted it with alacrity.

"I confess my throat was dry when I arrived here. It has not rained for weeks and the roads are very dusty."

While he was speaking, he was looking at Rosetta.

She was undoubtedly one of the most beautiful girls he had ever seen.

He had heard people talking about Dolina and yet because he had learnt she was little more than a *debutante*, he had not paid any attention.

Now he saw her, he thought she seemed older than her years or perhaps he had been misinformed about her age.

The brothers felt it would be a mistake to talk about the Racecourse the moment the Marquis arrived.

Therefore Gordon and Henry had put a light cloth over the plans and it would be, they decided, after dinner before they would really begin to discuss the matter with the Marquis.

In fact the Marquis was just about to enquire,

"Now tell me why you are so anxious to see me," just as Barnes announced,

"Dinner is served, my Lord."

"I confess to feeling hungry," the Marquis observed as they turned to the door. "His Royal Highness always has extremely good food at Marlborough House, but, as I missed my tea, I am looking forward to my dinner."

"Then we hope what we have to offer you will not be disappointing," Gordon remarked.

He led the way into the dining room and he was aware that the Marquis was scrutinising the shining silver on the table with appreciation in his eyes.

He did not say anything and, as Gordon had heard that the silver at The Castle was really amazing, he hoped that he would not despise theirs.

They sat down with Gordon at the top of the table with the Marquis on his right and Rosetta on his left and Henry on the other side of Rosetta.

"This is a charming room," the Marquis remarked.

He was looking at the pictures on the walls and the fine marble fireplace that had been brought from Rome by one of the Waincliffe ancestors.

"Anything we have," Gordon replied, "has always been overshadowed by all you have at The Castle. I have often thought that it was an unfair stroke of fate that we should be situated side by side."

"Well, at least our families have been friendly over the years," said the Marquis, "and indeed ever since they chose to live in this part of the country."

"That is true," added Rosetta. "In fact one of our many illustrious ancestors was known as 'Waincliffe the Good', and one of his Lordship's was 'Millbrook the Just'."

The Marquis chortled.

"I recall hearing that. What was he just about?"

"I expect he looked after his people and made sure they did not suffer injustice or unfairness," Rosetta replied. "If you remember, he was a judge for many years and even the highwaymen respected him, because he would never exaggerate the charges against them."

The Marquis stared at her in surprise.

"How do you know all this?" he asked.

"Living in the country, my Lord, I have naturally read about your family, just as I have read about ours in the archives."

"I have a suspicion," the Marquis said, "you know considerably more about my family than I know myself. I had completely forgotten the ancestor who was called 'the Just' or that he was a judge."

"I think the truth is," Gordon chipped in, "that you have very little time to think about your ancestors when you are enjoying yourself in London, while we, who live here quietly, have plenty of time to study the past as well as the present."

"I am most intrigued," said the Marquis, "that your sister should know so much about my family. Or was that particular Marquis more interesting than the others?"

He knew, as he spoke, that any woman with whom he was flirting in London would say at once that he, the present Marquis, was much the most interesting.

Instead of which Rosetta responded,

"My favourite of your family is the one who defied Cromwell's men. He was so brave in fighting against them that they deliberately left The Castle untouched despite its strategic position in the County."

"Is that true?" asked Gordon. "The Cromwellians did a great deal of damage to us."

"I have heard the story of the defence of The Castle since I was in the cradle," the Marquis replied. "But I am surprised it should have been of any interest to you, Miss Dolina."

"I love history, my Lord, and I would rather read about the past than any other subject and I study the history of other countries as well."

As he was listening, Gordon guessed that Rosetta's father must have taught her all this.

The Marquis was intrigued.

As he helped himself to the first course, he turned to Rosetta and asked,

"Tell me more, I want to hear what you know about my family, since you seem to know more than I do."

"I have not had the privilege of going round your Castle, my Lord, but I am told you own treasures that are finer and better than anything at Windsor Castle."

The Marquis laughed.

"I like to think so, but actually the Royal collection is superb, but I should like to hear your opinion on mine."

"I expect that what Dolina is really saying," Henry remarked, "is that she would like to go round The Castle. Do you realise that, although we live so near, none of us has ever been invited to your house."

"Is that true!" the Marquis exclaimed. "I thought you must have gone to parties there in my father's time or when I was away exploring the world."

"I hope that you remembered to write down all you discovered," Rosetta said, "and perhaps one day you will write a book about your tours, my Lord."

"If I did, do you think anyone would read it?"

"I am sure they would, especially as you are so well known and so often in the newspapers. Readers would be curious to learn about your adventures overseas."

The Marquis was sharp enough to be aware that she was not being particularly complimentary and in a way she was rebuking him for having such a smeared reputation.

It was something that he had never expected to hear from a pretty woman – least of all one who lived in the country.

He imagined that she would know nothing about his *affaires de coeur* and if she did, then she would be too shy to mention them.

"I think," he said, "you are challenging me to make myself more useful to humanity than I am at present."

"I feel sure that you are very charitable in your own way," Rosetta smiled softly. "Equally you must not expect us to know all about it here in the depths of the country."

The Marquis thought she was laughing at him and he became even more intrigued.

He had never met a woman without realising that the moment she saw him she was aware of him as a man.

Yet in a subtle manner this young girl, for she was little more, was challenging his brain rather than his looks.

He felt honour bound to protect himself.

"I tell you what I'll do," he proposed. "Tomorrow, when we have discussed the subject your brothers wish to raise with me, I will invite you all to The Castle. Then you will see for yourself if it is as wonderful as you believe it to be."

Henry gave a cry of delight.

"Do you really mean that? You have no idea how much I have always wanted to stand on the Tower and find out how far you can see from it. I have been told it is five Counties, but I would love to see for myself."

The Marquis chuckled.

"And so you shall. People who come to The Castle always find it fascinating."

"I want to see your collection of armour, which is always spoken of as being the best anywhere," Gordon added. "My father said that some of the weapons you own are not even in the Tower of London."

"You shall see them all! Now, Miss Dolina, what is your particular interest?"

"Almost everything you possess," Rosetta replied. "But I am especially anxious to know if the portrait you own of Queen Elizabeth, which I am told is the best ever painted of her, was done during her lifetime. I am afraid I don't know the name of the artist."

"Nicholas Hilliard and he painted it, I believe, in 1570."

"The Queen would have been thirty-seven then, and she must actually have sat for him!" exclaimed Rosetta.

She knew, as she spoke, that her father would be so delighted at this information and even if she discovered nothing else, it would give him great pleasure.

"I am wondering," the Marquis continued, "if you know that I have an even more important picture than that of Queen Elizabeth."

Rosetta smiled.

"I have been told," she said, "that Holbein's portrait of Henry VIII and his Court is the most striking Royal portrait in any collection, including the Queen's."

"You are right, of course you are right, but I am intrigued to find out how you know so much when you live here quietly in the country."

"We actually have quite a good library," Gordon said quickly, in case the Marquis was suspicious of Rosetta because she knew so much.

Gordon well knew that history had never interested Dolina and as far as he could remember, she had read only novels. She seldom went into the library, let alone read any of the books their family had acquired over the years.

"I feel sure that your sister will enjoy my library," the Marquis was saying. "My father was meticulous about buying old books at sales. I must admit I have been more interested in horses than in books."

"That is just the subject we intend to talk to you about," Henry began.

Even as he spoke, he realised Gordon was frowning at him.

Then, at that very moment, Barnes arrived with the second course and there was no doubt that Mrs. Barnes had really excelled herself.

When dinner was finished, the Marquis called out,

"Please give my compliments to the cook and tell her I have never enjoyed a meal more or eaten so much."

He had asked for second helpings of two dishes and Gordon felt that the kitchen would be dancing with delight at the compliment.

As the dinner came to an end, Rosetta suggested,

"As we are just a family party, I have no wish to leave you gentlemen to your port. I think, as it is late, it would be wise if we went back to the study and you told his Lordship, Gordon, why you have invited him here."

She looked at Gordon and he understood that she was worried that the Marquis would say he was tired and go off to bed and then perhaps in the morning there would not be enough time to discuss the Racecourse before he said he wished to leave for his Castle.

"Of course you are quite right," Gordon agreed.

As Rosetta rose to her feet, they all stood up too.

Gordon glanced at the clock on the mantelpiece as they left the dining room.

He felt that Rosetta was being very wise and, as he had been anxious for the Marquis to enjoy himself, he had not realised they had talked for so long about The Castle and that time was passing.

They walked down the passage.

As they did so, the Marquis was thinking that no one could be more graceful and elegant than his hostess.

He had, as he had said, heard her beauty acclaimed in London and he had only to open *The Court Circular* to realise she was at most of the fashionable parties.

He had merely thought of her as yet another young beauty who would doubtless be married off to some titled gentleman before the Season was out.

Perhaps in two or three years' time she would be of interest to him!

But, now he had seen her, he had to admit she was even lovelier than he expected and to his astonishment far more intelligent.

The *debutantes* once they became married women were usually, he had found, extremely dull with little or nothing to talk about.

The older women with whom he had spent his time were certainly not readers of history and they had no wish to talk of anything else but themselves and love.

They walked into the study to see that Barnes had lit more candles than usual.

When Gordon entered the room, he saw that he had taken the cover off the plans and there were extra candles round that table.

He moved towards it and gestured with his hands.

"This is the reason I asked you, my Lord, to come here. I think you will see at a glance exactly what it is."

As he spoke, he drew in his breath.

It was almost like putting his head on a block.

He would know in the next minute or so whether the Marquis was interested or not.

The Marquis walked to the table and stared down at the plans and then he exclaimed,

"This is a Racecourse! I don't know exactly what you want me to say about it."

"I want you to look at it closely, my Lord, because this is what my brother and I want to build on our land and yours."

The Marquis gazed at Gordon and then at the plan.

"On your land and mine," he echoed in a strange tone, "but why?"

"First of all because it lends itself completely to a Racecourse and because Henry and I need the profits to keep our house going. We think it could also be of great benefit to the whole County."

"I have often heard people grumble because there is not one, but I never thought of building one myself."

"I should have thought," Rosetta said very quietly, "it might have occurred to you, if you remember that your first ancestor to build The Castle, arranged races. Not of horses but of men."

The Marquis turned to look at her.

"That is true, but I had not thought about it in a long time. And the steeplechases we have occasionally are very different from a Racecourse."

"But you do see that this is what is needed today," Rosetta interposed, "because you and Gordon have superb horses and apart from your enjoyment, the people round here have to go a very long distance to find a Racecourse of any sort."

"I really think that it's far too big a project for me to consider at the moment," the Marquis began.

As Gordon and Henry drew in their breath, thinking that they had failed, Rosetta countered,

"I don't think, my Lord, you have considered the feelings of your neighbours and the people living on your estate."

"What do you mean by that?" the Marquis enquired in a somewhat hostile tone.

"There are few amusements in this County, except in the winter. Even the hunting and shooting cannot make up for the very long months when there is nothing to see, nothing to make people socialise with each other or for that matter to talk about."

The Marquis laughed.

"I cannot believe that."

"It's true," Rosetta persisted, "and what I believe is so much more important, is that people in the villages are getting poorer and poorer by the year. I think the building of a Racecourse would mean a great deal to them and they would naturally look to you, my Lord, for leadership."

She paused, but the Marquis did not speak and she went on,

"There could be many new visitors coming into the County, new shops and new hotels simply because of the Race Meetings."

The Marquis made a murmur, so she added quickly,

"It would attract people down from London as well as those who never cross our borders as there is nothing particular here to interest them."

She spoke in a manner that not only surprised the Marquis, but made it impossible for him not to listen to her.

She was pleading with him, but at the same time, he was well aware that she was telling him it was his duty.

It was an idea he should have thought of himself and tonight was something that had never happened to him before.

He realised he could almost read Rosetta's thoughts and he could sense that she was thinking he was selfish and indifferent to those dependant upon him.

He turned away from her gaze to look down at the plans again and then he enquired politely,

"Tell me exactly where this is on your estate and where does it come into mine."

Gordon took a pencil from the writing table and, as he did so, Rosetta moved closer to the Marquis.

"This is Monkswood here," she pointed to the plan. "This side of Monkswood is where you shoot. Although it is some way from The Castle, you would have an excellent view of the Racecourse from your Tower."

"How do you know?" the Marquis asked sharply.

"Because I can use my eyes, my Lord. When I was riding, and I admit trespassing, over your land last week, I was thinking what an excellent view you have of the land that lies in front of you, but what a pity that it is absolutely barren without even a house or cottage on it."

"I like it that way," the Marquis replied stubbornly.

"A Racecourse would only enhance your view and it would cause no trouble to you if all the villages beyond your gates became more prosperous and increased their population."

She waited for him to reply and then she added,

"Meadowfield village is now so short of inhabitants that the Vicar of Little Sowerby goes to the Church there only once a month."

"What you are really saying, is that I am neglecting my estate and the people who live on it!"

"You have not exactly neglected them, my Lord, but because they feel isolated a great number have moved away. People do like living in villages, but it must be a comfortable and prosperous village with at least two shops so that they don't have to go long distances for everything they need.

"At Flagford and Little Corner there are a number of empty cottages becoming dilapidated and I know that several shops in both of them are thinking of closing down, which means that more inhabitants will leave."

The Marquis was silent and then he blurted out,

"I had no idea of any of this."

"Why should you bother about our local troubles here when you are having a good time in London?" Rosetta asked. "Everything would undoubtedly change if we had a Race Meeting here perhaps three or four times a year."

There was silence and then Henry broke in,

"Of course, it would be wonderful for our horses, and we could have super high jumps, whilst at present we have to make do with hedges and a few old hurdles.

The Marquis was staring at the plan.

"Have you any idea what this will cost?" he asked.

"It would depend on whether we build as much as possible ourselves with local labour or call in an expensive outside Company," replied Gordon.

He was looking rather pale and Rosetta knew that he was thinking their prospects were hopeless.

"It would be best," the Marquis said slowly, "if we employed local people where possible. They would take more interest in it as they would feel part of it."

"That is right! Of course it's right!" Rosetta cried before anyone else could speak. "It's what they would all love to do and it would give them new interests, new ideas and, above all, hope."

"*Hope*?" the Marquis questioned.

"Hope that the future will be better than it seems at present. It's what everyone wants in their hearts, but so often they are disappointed."

As she was speaking, their eyes met.

The Marquis thought that she was the most unusual young woman he had ever met.

He had never imagined anyone so beautiful could talk so seriously and with so much commonsense and he was fully aware that what she was saying was true.

He felt he should have known all this, but he had thought such matters were not particularly his business and had refused to let them trouble him.

And now, it seemed incredible, she was reading his thoughts.

Then Rosetta declared,

"Every young man is entitled to sow his wild oats, but there is a time when he recognises his responsibilities and that people whom he thought of no importance look to him for guidance and a lead."

"You think," the Marquis answered slowly, "that is what they are asking of me?"

"Yes, it is, my Lord. You live in that wonderful Castle. But the people to whom you belong and who have fought and died for your ancestors are now seeking your help. You can give them it in a very special way and if you do, they will be eternally grateful."

Once again the Marquis was looking at her.

He was thinking it could not be possible for anyone so young and so beautiful to be talking to him in such a manner.

Then he could see in her eyes how much it mattered to her and she was undoubtedly thinking not of herself, as any other woman would be, but of him and his people.

He turned to the plan.

"If I agree to this," he said, "how soon could you start and how long would it take?"

Gordon, who had been looking despondent, seemed to suddenly come to life.

"Henry and I have worked out rough answers to all those questions and I have written them down in case you wanted to take them away and consider them."

He picked up a sheet of paper from his writing desk and handed it to the Marquis, who took a brief glance at it.

"I suppose you and your brother are prepared to be in charge all the time the Racecourse is being built. I am sure I will be able to find friends who would contribute to the more elaborate part of the course and I know someone who specialises in building the most comfortable stands."

Gordon drew a deep breath.

"Are you really saying you will help us in this?"

The Marquis looked towards Rosetta.

"After what your sister has just said to me, I find it difficult to say 'no'."

Rosetta clasped her hands together.

"Thank you, thank you, my Lord. This is the most wonderful news. I know that everyone will feel you are following in the steps of the greatest and most popular of your ancestors. You will give the local people, who are all *our* people, something to think about, to plan for and to give them employment."

"Very well," the Marquis sighed, "you go ahead. I imagine that, if you move quickly, we ought to be able to have our first Race Meeting early next year."

Gordon gave an exclamation of delight.

"Do you really mean that you will do it, my Lord? We have to be frank and say that Henry and I can, at the moment, only offer you the land and ourselves."

"You must supervise the whole of it and make sure it is the most outstanding in the country. If you do that, I am prepared to pay all the costs and we will then share the profits when we make any."

Rosetta spoke first.

"That is very kind and generous of you," she said. "I know that when our people hear of it they will thank you from the bottom of their hearts."

"I rather doubt that. There will certainly be a great number of critics," the Marquis replied rather cynically.

Rosetta shook her head.

"You have no idea how much the Millbrooks are revered. The locals are only disappointed that you spend so little time here. If they know you are really caring about us who live here and bringing much needed prosperity to the County, I am quite certain they will canonize you!"

The Marquis laughed.

"Now you are really frightening me! I have no wish to be a Saint and I enjoy life as I find it."

As he spoke, he knew that this was not true, as he had been disappointed in what he had found in London.

This was a new idea, a new project, on his own land and near his own house.

Unless he had arranged a party he had often found The Castle exceedingly boring, but now he might find a happiness and interest he had failed to discover in London.

As if she knew what he was thinking, Rosetta said very quietly,

"You will never regret the decision you have made, my Lord. I promise you greater happiness than anything you have ever known before."

The Marquis stared at her.

What she had just said implied that she had been reading his mind.

He could not believe it.

Then he was aware that she had been speaking in a very low voice and her brothers, who were concentrating on the plan, would not have heard what she said to him.

For a moment they just looked at each other and then the Marquis murmured,

"What part will you play in this, apart from making me do *exactly* what you want me to do?"

"You have done the right thing, my Lord."

She did not answer his question, but turned away towards the side table where Barnes had left another bottle of champagne on ice.

"I think," she announced, "we should all drink to the Racecourse that has been born here tonight and which we must make one of the best courses in England."

"Indeed we must," Henry agreed excitedly. "But I am finding it hard to believe it will really happen. Oh, my Lord, you will be the most popular Millbrook who has ever lived at The Castle."

Because Henry was so thrilled the Marquis laughed and Gordon handed him a glass of champagne.

Having poured one out for Rosetta and Henry, he replenished his own.

"I want you," he proposed, "to drink a toast to the Millbrook and Waincliffe Racecourse. I suggest it is called 'Millcliffe', which would unite our two names in the same way as we are the united proprietors of the course."

Just for a moment, the Marquis paused as if he was considering it.

Then raising his glass, he added,

"I will drink to that. I will drink to the Millcliffe Racecourse, and to the beautiful lady who will watch over it as its Guardian Angel sent down from Heaven!"

He was looking at Rosetta as he spoke.

Henry and Gordon lifted their glasses repeating,

"To the Millcliffe Racecourse."

Then as they were downing the champagne, Rosetta moved swiftly out of the room and disappeared.

CHAPTER FIVE

Rosetta woke up with a start and then she realised it was still very early.

It was not yet six o'clock.

For a moment she just lay in bed.

She could see, as the wardrobe door was open, the gown she had worn last night.

They had gone up to change for dinner at half past seven although the Marquis had not arrived and at the back of their minds was the fear that he would not turn up at all.

And that would be the end of the Racecourse!

To cheer herself up, Rosetta had then chosen one of Dolina's prettiest gowns. It was pale pink and ornamented with diamante and flowers and it gave her the feeling when she put it on that she was the Fairy Queen of the garden.

When the Marquis did arrive, she had no idea that was exactly how she looked to him. He was astonished to see anyone so lovely or so well dressed in the country.

Now it swept over Rosetta like a wave of the sea that everything was even better than they had hoped. The Marquis would cooperate with them and actually finance the construction of the Racecourse.

'We have won! We have won!' she told herself.

She felt as if even the sunshine was brighter as it came streaming through the sides of the curtains.

Last night when they had gone up to bed, Gordon had escorted the Marquis to his room and then he came to Rosetta's to say goodnight.

She was sitting at the dressing table taking off her jewellery.

"I cannot begin to thank you," he said. "What can I give you as a present for being so brilliant?"

"I can answer that quite easily," replied Rosetta. "I would love a ride on Starlight."

"I might have known that would be your answer and he is yours for tomorrow if you really think you can control him."

"I will be very disappointed if I fail!"

He thanked her again and she climbed into her bed feeling that the angels had helped them and everything was even more wonderful than she had hoped it would be.

As it was so early, Rosetta thought that she would take Gordon at his word and ride Starlight now.

There was always a chance that the situation might change or Dolina might come home and then she would have to return to her own home very quickly.

'It's now or never,' she told herself and jumped out of bed.

As she saw it was going to be a hot day, she put on her riding skirt and a white blouse, but not her riding jacket and she guessed that if Starlight was obstreperous, the less she wore the easier it would be to control him.

She dressed very quickly and opened her bedroom door to find everything in the house was quiet.

There was no sign of any servants.

In the past when there were a great number of them, she was sure that the housemaids and the scullions would be on duty at five-thirty, but now the staff were old.

Rosetta remembered that before they went upstairs, Gordon had said that breakfast would be at nine o'clock.

She slipped out by the back door and onto the path that led her directly to the stables.

As she expected, there was no sign yet of any of the grooms and even most of the horses were still lying down.

It was not difficult to find Starlight.

She wanted to view and pat the Marquis's horses, which had broken the record yesterday, but she thought the sooner she rode off on Starlight the less likely it was for anyone to stop her from doing so.

He was quiet while she saddled and bridled him and then leading him out of the stable into the yard she climbed onto the mounting block.

She seated herself in the saddle and she had been talking to Starlight all the time.

Her father had taught her years ago when she was a child that one should always talk to a horse, especially a new one as it made it familiar with its rider before he or she was actually in the saddle.

"You are a very beautiful and clever boy," Rosetta was saying. "I want to ride you because I think you are without any exception the loveliest horse I have ever seen."

She was sure that Starlight understood that she was praising him.

She patted him and he set off at quite a reasonable pace instead, as she had expected, of trying to go too fast.

They went out of the back of the stable and into the paddock and then she let him break into a gallop and she thought it was the most exciting thing she had done for a long time.

She rode him out of the paddock towards the land Gordon and Henry had planned for their Racecourse.

But she did not want to spoil the excitement of riding over it with the Marquis later, so she turned towards Monkswood, her favourite place on the whole estate.

As it happened, Monkswood had always been of some significance as half of it was on the Marquis's estate and half on Lord Waincliffe's.

Nearly a hundred years ago there had been a tussle between the two owners as to who owned Monkswood and strangely enough the event was chronicled in the archives of both families.

It was of special interest locally because a monk had left his Monastery and then retired to the wood and had built himself a small Chapel.

There he had meditated all alone talking only to the birds and rabbits and other wild animals. He not only fed them, but offered them the protection of his Chapel.

Whether or not they did really hide in the Chapel when the owners of Monkswood were shooting, Rosetta was never sure, but she liked to think of them all clustering inside it.

The Chapel was now very dilapidated, but she felt it still had an atmosphere of sanctity about it.

She thought now as she rode through the wood that she should say a prayer of gratitude to God for making the Marquis agree to the building of the Racecourse, and it was appropriate it should be here in the wood that had been part of the two estates for centuries.

She did not want Starlight to be too frisky while they were inside the wood, so she galloped him on their way to it and took him over several very high jumps that he cleared magnificently.

He was, she told him, the most marvellous horse she had ever ridden.

She had no idea that the Marquis was watching her take the jumps with sheer astonishment.

He too had woken early.

He had lain in bed thinking that he had certainly let himself in for a project he had never even thought about.

He was wondering if in some subtle way he could persuade Gordon Waincliffe it was not really wanted.

Then, almost as if she was standing beside him, he could hear the soft clear voice of Dolina.

She was telling him that it was his duty as well as his responsibility and that he must do his best to help his own people.

She had certainly managed to convince him.

He thought now with a sigh it meant he would have to spend a lot more time in the country, far more than he had done in the last few years.

Then he saw the sun coming through the window and heard a bird singing outside.

He felt a sudden urge to look at the place chosen for the Racecourse and if there were to be snags, he must find them now and then if he decided the whole scheme was impossible, he must have very good reasons for saying so.

So without waiting for his valet, he pulled on his riding breeches and a shirt.

When he was dressed, he went downstairs and just as Rosetta had found, there was no one around.

He let himself out of the front door and walked round to the stables, expecting his groom, if no one else, to be on duty, but obviously no one had thought that he would be awake and active at such an early hour.

Just as Rosetta had done, the Marquis saddled one of his own horses and he was thinking, as he did so, he had chosen the best of his magical team.

He then rode into the paddock and only then did he notice that a groom had appeared at the other end of the cobbled yard, yawning as he did so.

The Marquis rode away and following his instinct, he rounded the house and garden.

Then he was in a field in the right direction for the area where the Racecourse was to be built.

As he did so and looked down into the valley, the horse he was riding began galloping, almost instinctively the Marquis thought, in the direction of The Castle.

Because he was already enjoying his ride, he gave the horse its head. He wanted to see how fast it could cover the ground that fortunately was not soft or boggy.

He had galloped for quite some way before he saw ahead of him that there was another rider, who was at that moment putting his horse over what appeared to be a very high and dangerous jump.

Yet that horse landed without any difficulty at all and started off in the direction of another jump.

It was then that the Marquis became aware that the rider was sitting sidesaddle and obviously was a woman.

He could hardly believe his eyes as the first jump was so very high – and so was the second. He would have hesitated before attempting either of them with the mount he was riding.

Feeling curious, he rode towards her and soon saw to his great astonishment who it was – the girl who had, he thought, pushed him last night into committing himself to something he had never even considered before.

Then Rosetta sailed over the second jump in the same brilliant way she had managed the first.

The Marquis felt, as he had last night, that she was the most extraordinary young woman he had ever met.

How could she ride as she was riding now, he asked himself, looking so soft and feminine and seeming almost ethereal rather than just human?

As he drew nearer, he could see she was patting her horse and she was quite obviously making a fuss of him because he had performed so well.

And then without looking back, she set off towards Monkswood.

The Marquis followed her.

As she was now not riding so fast, he was slowly catching her up.

The Marquis's antecedents and the Lord Waincliffe of the time had agreed together that they would each have the use of Monkswood, but the Marquis seldom shot there. He had concentrated on making the woods on the other side of The Castle better for holding his pheasants.

His half of Monkswood had been neglected and he had never wondered if the present Lord Waincliffe ever used his right to intrude on The Castle half of the wood, but he had never been particularly interested in it and had wasted no time making enquiries.

Now, as Rosetta disappeared amongst the trees, he thought it might be a bit difficult to find her.

Fortunately, however, there was, although he had not seen it before, a path leading into the very heart of the wood.

When the Marquis reached the path, he had a quick glimpse of the girl moving ahead of him.

He rode on and then he came to what he supposed was actually the centre of the wood and in a clearing there was a small pool surrounded by kingcups.

Rosetta was dismounting.

As he appeared, she turned round.

He saw by the surprise in her eyes she had no idea that he had been following her.

He rode up to her and then he dismounted as well.

"I never expected to see you here, my Lord," she said, "and so early in the morning."

"I had a desire, as you must have had," the Marquis replied, "to be out in the sunshine. That is an exceedingly fine horse you are riding."

"It belongs to Gordon. When he asked if he could give me a present, I told him the one thing I wanted was to ride Starlight."

"So that is his name and one he certainly deserves. I have been watching you jump and I had no idea that any ordinary horse could take such high jumps, especially if it was ridden by a woman!"

Rosetta laughed.

"In some ways we can be as good as a man and, as it happens, I have not ridden a finer horse than Starlight."

"I am not surprised. Still I can hardly believe that you were brave enough to take him over such high jumps."

"I could not resist it. My own horse, much as I love him, could never have attempted anything so high. Nor could he have galloped as fast as Starlight has just done."

"I was watching you, Dolina, and I am puzzled why you have come here. Is there something special about it?"

"Of course there is, my Lord. Surely you are aware of it."

She pointed behind him with her hand.

When he turned to look, he saw that there in the middle of the wood was a small dilapidated building and for a moment he wondered why it should interest her.

Then he exclaimed,

"Of course! That was where the old monk lived! I remember being told about it when I was a small boy."

"Yes, that was where he lived and where he fed the birds, the squirrels and the rabbits. Usually when I come here, I bring them food just as they were given all that time ago by the monk."

The Marquis smiled sardonically.

It was the sort of thing, he reflected, she would do.

He could not possibly imagine any woman of his acquaintance bothering about anything as mundane as birds and squirrels especially when they might be talking to him.

"I have come here this morning," Rosetta said in a very soft voice, "to say a prayer of gratitude that you are building the Racecourse. I have a feeling that it was the monk who changed your mind when you were just about to say 'no'."

"I think rather it was *you* who changed my mind," the Marquis countered.

"At any rate it was the monk who has always loved this wood and who I believe has blessed our side as well as yours."

"Can you really go safely inside that building?" the Marquis asked. "It looks as though it needs a great deal of attention."

"That is another thing I have longed for," Rosetta said. "But, as we cannot afford to repair our own ceilings which are falling down for want of attention, it is not likely there would be enough money to repair the Chapel."

"Are you suggesting this is another cause I should undertake?" the Marquis quizzed her.

Rosetta shook her head.

"No, it's definitely not your business. Not unless the Racecourse is such a huge success that you feel you

93

must thank someone and who better than the monk who inspired it?"

She spoke with such sincerity that he sensed she believed in every word she was saying.

As she tied Starlight's bridle to a bough of a fallen tree, he did the same with his horse.

Rosetta glanced at him as he did so, but she did not say anything and when she turned to walk towards the little Chapel, the Marquis followed her.

It was larger inside than he had expected, although half the roof had fallen in and the windows were broken.

Yet it was easy to see that it had once been a small Chapel and it was a miracle it had survived for so long.

The floor was covered with moss and although the stone altar was still there, there was no cross.

The Marquis unexpectedly found himself, just like Rosetta, conscious of a feeling of sanctity.

As they entered, a number of small birds flew from the beams out through what had once been a window.

There were small creatures scurrying over the floor and they disappeared either out of the Chapel or into the overgrown weeds.

The Marquis stared about him.

Then Rosetta went down on her knees in front of the altar and he could see that she was praying fervently.

Her eyes were closed and her hands were clasped together.

She made, with her curly fair hair and white blouse, a picture the Marquis felt was incredibly moving – and so beautiful that any artist would find it irresistible.

It was a good long time since he had seen a woman praying or had been with one who was so oblivious of him personally that she did not even turn round to see if he was kneeling behind her.

When she raised her head with her eyes still shut, a bright shaft of glorious light seemed to stream in through the battered window over the altar.

For a moment it turned her hair to gold.

And it enveloped her as if it was a blessing from God Himself.

As the Marquis then drew in his breath, unable to believe what he was witnessing, Rosetta rose to her feet.

Smiling at him, she said,

"I have thanked the monk. I know he will bless the Racecourse and it will be a huge success."

Without waiting for him to answer, she walked out of the Chapel towards the horses.

Starlight was straining against his ties and, as she released him, she turned to the Marquis,

"When I come here on my own horse, he is so well trained that he just waits for me without being tied up."

Even as she spoke, she realised that she had made a bloomer – she had spoken not as Dolina but as herself.

She hoped, however, the Marquis was not listening to her or thought her remark in any way strange.

When she turned again towards him, he picked her up in his arms and set her on Starlight's saddle and then as she began to ride slowly back along the path, he mounted his own horse and followed her.

It was impossible for them to talk, as the path was very narrow and the Marquis was obliged to ride behind her and, instead of going out of the wood the way she had come in, she suddenly turned to the left.

Soon the Marquis was aware that they were on the ground on which the Racecourse would be built.

It was quite flat over a large area and he knew there would be no reason to disturb Monkswood, although there were some small copses that would have to be demolished, but otherwise it was a natural site for a Racecourse.

The Marquis then drew alongside her, saying,

"It looks most attractive just as it is – "

Rosetta glanced at him, then realised he was teasing her, enjoying his own little joke.

"A gentleman's word is his bond," she retorted just slightly sternly.

"You can hardly suspect me of going back on all I promised last night. Also you have just sealed it with a blessing from Heaven and anyway I am far too cowardly to defy anything so masterful as your prayers!"

"I am very glad of that, my Lord, and you do have to admit it's all very exciting and something so different from what has ever happened in this part of the world."

"I think the historians would disagree with you, but I am quite sure that, if nothing else, Dolina, you have given our people something to talk about – "

He glanced at Rosetta before he finished,

"*Instead of me!*"

She gave a little laugh.

"I wondered if you realised that you are the prime topic of conversation from the highest to the lowest in this County."

"I would imagine that they have nothing better to interest them, but it has never troubled me what they say or don't say. And I am very glad that you are not despising me as much as you did when I arrived last night."

Rosetta looked at him in surprise.

"What made you think that?" she asked.

"Perhaps I am perceptive when it concerns myself, but I sense your thoughts and your feelings and they are so different from any I have received from a pretty woman."

"But now, in a few months, you are going to be the most popular man who has ever lived at The Castle!"

The Marquis laughed, but he did not reply at once.

After a moment, he asked Rosetta,

"Shall we race our horses? I think the winning post should be that tree you can just see on the horizon."

"You tell me when to start, my Lord."

They drew in their horses, as the Marquis intoned,

"One, two, three – go!"

They swept forward.

Even as they did so, the Marquis realised that she was without exception the most brilliant female rider he had ever known.

In addition Starlight was indeed an exceptionally fine thoroughbred and he was carrying, the Marquis knew, a much lighter weight that his mount was bearing.

They were neck-and-neck until shortly before they reached the tree he had selected for the winning post.

By an almost superhuman effort Rosetta managed almost to pass him.

It was then that the Marquis by sheer outstanding riding drew level with her just as they reached the tree.

"A dead heat!" he exclaimed as they pulled in their mounts.

"I thought for a moment I was going to beat you," Rosetta exclaimed. "But you are too good a rider. In fact, without exaggeration I can say I have never known a man ride as well as you do."

"That is exactly what I was going to say to you. In fact for a woman you are terrific and there is no other word for it, Dolina."

"I think you should really say that to Starlight. It's extremely easy to be a good rider when you are on a superb horse and far more difficult when your horse does its best but is really not, as you might say, first class."

She was thinking of her own beloved stallion as she spoke and as he was growing older he would not have been able to compete as she had done with the Marquis's horse.

"I would say one thing," the Marquis said quietly, "that, while we are building the Racecourse, you must have entrée to my stables."

He thought as he spoke that it would please Rosetta more than anything else he could offer her.

She turned to look at him as if to question whether he really meant it and then he saw the light and excitement in her eyes that he felt were very touching.

Then, for no reason he could understand, she turned away and replied to him in a rather strange tone,

"That is very kind of you, my Lord, and of course I am most grateful."

Because he was so perceptive, the Marquis knew at once that something was wrong and yet he did not have any idea what it could be.

How could he possibly know that for one moment Rosetta had felt as if he carried her up into the sky.

And then she had remembered he was speaking not to her but to Dolina.

It would be Dolina who would be able to ride his horses – *not her.*

She was already resigning herself to the fact that, once the work began on the Racecourse, she would have to make herself very scarce.

It meant of course that she would have to ride in the opposite direction to where either the Marquis or Gordon and Henry were likely to be.

It would be fatal if he caught a glimpse of her when Dolina was at home.

They rode in silence for a short distance and then Rosetta remarked,

"I think we should be going back. It must be nearly time for breakfast and I know that the boys will be wanting to talk to you."

"For the moment I am quite content to talk to you," the Marquis replied. "And I am much looking forward to showing you my Castle this afternoon, Dolina."

"And I am looking forward to seeing it, my Lord. If it is anything like as marvellous as I am told it is, then it will be very difficult to make ourselves concentrate on the Racecourse. So we should get that over this morning."

"There are so many things I want to show you and ask your opinion on that I am sure some of them will have to be left for another day."

There was silence for a moment and then Rosetta commented rather provocatively,

"What will they do in London if you stay too long in the country and give them nothing to talk about?"

"Now you are being unkind to me. I am well aware I am talked about, but I have no wish for you to look at me as you did last night. So naturally I will have to mend my ways and spend my time concentrating on the Racecourse."

Rosetta laughed.

"I am quite certain you will do nothing of the sort. As I have already said, if you suddenly become obsessed by the country, *London* will have nothing to gossip about, whilst we will have you for breakfast, luncheon, tea and dinner!"

The Marquis thought that the way she teased him was something he had not known for many years.

Women had always loaded him with compliments, or else were pleading almost frantically for expressions of love from him.

"If you say much more," he said, "I will spend all the money I have to spare on building myself a Church where I can repent of my sins and the Racecourse will have to be forgotten!"

"That is cheating, my Lord. At the moment the Racecourse is far more important for us than any Church could be for you."

"That is your opinion, Dolina, but of course I am entitled to mine."

"You will have to be very astute and very subtle to convert me!" Rosetta answered.

The Marquis thought again how different she was in every way from any woman he had ever known.

Now they were fencing verbally with each other and making it, he considered, far more amusing than any conversation he had ever had with any female.

The Hall was now in sight and he suggested,

"I think before you exhaust your mind trying to get the better of me, we should now exhaust our bodies with another race. How about it, Dolina!"

Rosetta's eyes lit up.

"We have about half a mile ahead of us and so I challenge Starlight to reach the gate into the orchard before I reach it!"

Rosetta gave him a smile that seemed to illuminate her whole enchanting face.

Then her head was down and she was galloping Starlight away from him.

The Marquis caught her up.

At the gate, it was once again a dead heat.

"I thought I had won," Rosetta sighed.

"Fate has answered the question quite clearly," the Marquis observed. "We are inseparable."

Even as he spoke, he thought that Hermione or any of the other beauties would undoubtedly have made the most of that statement.

Whereas Dolina, as an unmarried girl, might read into his words something he had never said and, for the time being, never intended to say to anyone.

But Rosetta merely smiled.

"If we have the chance tomorrow," she said, "I am certain if it comes to a question of endurance that Starlight would beat your horse. That is what I will be thinking tomorrow if you are still with us at The Hall."

The Marquis had forgotten that he was supposed to be returning to The Castle later in the day.

He had been thinking that his valet could take over his clothes when Lord Waincliffe and his brother and sister had his conducted tour round The Castle.

Then, as Rosetta rode on ahead of him towards the stables, he really wanted to challenge her again.

He would feel dismal and bored if, after the visit to The Castle was over, they went home and he had to dine alone.

*

Back at The Hall Rosetta went up to her room and changed into one of the gowns belonging to Dolina.

She felt she had never enjoyed a morning more.

And the Marquis had not been at all as aloof and formidable as she had feared last night. This morning he seemed younger and considerably more amusing than she had expected him to be.

'Perhaps,' she told herself as she changed, 'he is not as bad as he is painted.'

But he would soon grow bored with being in the country with only the Racecourse to think about.

She wondered if Gordon would ask him to sign a document to confirm that he would pay for the costs – and whether they could trust him not to back out.

After all, they would be doing a great deal of work and spending money they could never recover.

Then she told herself that she did not believe for a moment the Marquis could behave like that and she would certainly expect him to be honourable and keep his word.

'At the same time,' she thought, 'it would be nice to make sure that everything is clear and tied-up and next she wondered if she ought to tell Gordon what she was thinking.

When she went downstairs to the breakfast room, the boys were already there talking nineteen to the dozen to the Marquis and they all rose when she entered.

"Please don't move," she asked them.

Then turning to Gordon, she exclaimed,

"Thank you so much for the most wonderful ride I had on Starlight. He is indeed marvellous and although his Lordship did his best to beat him, it was a dead heat."

"The Marquis has been telling us how you raced each other," said Henry. "And he is now determined to challenge us all with the new horses he intends to buy."

Rosetta looked at the Marquis enquiringly and he explained,

"There was a most fantastic collection coming up for sale at Tattersall's that belonged to a man who has just died. I was determined they would be mine and to my delight I heard yesterday, just before leaving London, that the executors have decided to accept the offer I made for the whole collection and they are being delivered to The Castle this morning."

"Oh, how fantastic!" cried Rosetta.

"I have seen them on several occasions when I was staying at their late owner's house. I always thought that they were the finest thoroughbreds I have ever seen."

"Now all your other poor horses at The Castle will take second place," said Rosetta. "I feel so sorry for them and I am sure they will feel hurt."

"In that case you will just have to look after them as well as all the people in my villages, Dolina. You could cheer them up by riding them."

He felt that her blue eyes would then shine with excitement as they had done before.

But to his surprise, she did not answer.

She merely walked to the side table to help herself from one of the silver dishes.

"Now today, my Lord," Henry came in excitedly, "we have to go to the Racecourse and show you exactly how it will look when it is finished."

"I was there this morning and I think you are quite right and have chosen just the right place for it."

"I thought if we rode there after breakfast," Gordon said, "we could decide exactly where the Racecourse itself should be as well as the paddock and the stands."

"I think," the Marquis added quietly, "we should have an expert to decide that. I happen to know the man in charge of Ascot Racecourse. I will ask him to come and answer all those questions that quite frankly I don't feel we are capable of answering ourselves."

"You are right," agreed Gordon, "and I think that we will all want to ride out this morning and will then be irresistibly drawn to where the Racecourse will be."

"I think Starlight should have a rest," said Rosetta. "I rode him rather hard this morning and he not only raced but excelled himself at the jumps."

Gordon looked at her in surprise.

"Are you telling me that you took him over what we call, 'the jumps' and which I have only just attempted to take myself?"

"He flew over them all like a bird and his Lordship was, I believe, impressed by his performance."

"I certainly was, Dolina, and, as I have many horses at The Castle that need exercising, why don't we go over there and instead of riding your horses, you can ride mine. You will actually be doing me a favour."

"It's certainly the best idea I ever heard," Henry enthused. "I have been longing to see the horses in your stable, my Lord. Whenever I have seen them on the roads or in the fields, I felt that they were too good to be true."

The Marquis smiled.

"Well, they are indeed true and I will be delighted to mount you all. What I suggest is that I drive Dolina, while you, Gordon and Henry, ride your own horses as far as my stables."

He deliberately used their Christian names and, as if he knew they were slightly surprised, he declared,

"After all, we are neighbours and now partners and we have known each other since we were children. Thus we cannot go on being so formal and, as you all know, my name is 'Euan'."

"I think that's marvellous, Euan," Gordon replied. "Then after luncheon you can show us The Castle, as you have promised."

"Then everything is arranged. All we have to do now is to wait for Dolina to change once again into her riding clothes."

Rosetta jumped up from the table.

"I promise to be no more than five minutes. I think that seeing your stables and your superb horses will be *so* exciting."

Now the Marquis could see her eyes shining.

He thought it impossible for any woman to look so thrilled – unless of course she was thinking about him!

"Hurry!" Henry called as Rosetta walked towards the door. "Otherwise Euan may change his mind and we will never see those marvellous horses except on canvas!"

The Marquis laughed.

"We will avoid that disaster," Rosetta piped up, "and I will be ready in three minutes instead of five!"

She ran from the room and the Marquis thought, as he had thought so many times already, that she was unique and so different from other women.

He could not imagine Hermione or any of the other beauties being so thrilled at the idea of riding his horses.

They kept their excitement for being with him and he knew only too well the way their lips invited his and the soft touch of their hands.

'She is just so unlike them in every way,' he told himself. 'As well as being the most beautiful girl I have ever seen.'

Then he asked himself why she did not respond to him as a man as every other woman did.

They had been together this morning, had talked and even prayed in the monk's Chapel.

Yet she still did not look at him invitingly.

He knew only too well there was not the expression in her eyes that told him she was longing for his kisses.

'Why, why,' he asked silently, as they rose from the breakfast table, 'is she so different?'

CHAPTER SIX

Driving behind the Marquis's magnificent team he had brought down from London, Rosetta thought it was an experience she had never had before.

The horses moved with a swiftness and smoothness she felt was fantastic and she found it hard to take her eyes off them.

She was looking exceedingly pretty in another of Dolina's dresses and a little hat that framed her face.

Once again, the Marquis thought that it gave her a unique ethereal look he had never seen before on any other woman.

Although it was just a short distance across country between The Hall and The Castle, it was several miles by road and they could not go fast all the time because of the villages they had to pass through.

Rosetta said nothing, but the Marquis noticed that she was looking at the empty cottages as they passed them and on most of them the thatch urgently needed restoring.

"If you are criticising me," the Marquis said as they passed by another cottage, "I can only tell you that I have seldom driven along these lanes before, so I am as shocked as you are at the amount of work that needs to be done in these villages."

She turned to smile at him as she replied,

"That is exactly what I want you to say. I know that once the Racecourse is built, people will flock to these villages and they will become prosperous overnight."

"Not as quickly as that, but you have made it very clear to me that I have neglected these people and must, of course, make amends."

"It's all so exciting, Euan, that I find it hard to think of anything else."

"If you don't like my Castle, I shall be extremely annoyed – "

"Of course I will like it. I have thought about it for years and wanted to see inside. I feel that this is a day I will always remember however old I become."

The Marquis laughed.

"I don't think you need worry about it at present, Dolina!"

He was just about to pay her a compliment and then he realised once again that she was watching the horses and it seemed to him so extraordinary that she should pay more attention to his horses than to him.

He had originally thought of her as just one of the many beauties of Mayfair, who were far more interested in London than the country.

In fact, he could not remember being with a woman who had no wish to live anywhere but in the middle of London – most of them would complain bitterly when they had to go to their husband's country seat.

To them the parties that took place in London every night were irresistible as well as all the luncheons when the food and wine were superlative and the balls where they could dance closely with him.

"I think the horse you were riding this morning," Rosetta butted into his thoughts, "is the best of the four, although they are all stupendous."

"That is what I thought, but I am surprised that you recognised it when they are all so perfectly matched."

"Even the horses have their special beauties," she remarked, "and no horse, even if their coats are the same colour, looks exactly like any other."

Rosetta was still admiring the team as they drove in at the gates that led to The Castle.

As they went up the drive, the Marquis could see that she was really elated at seeing his home.

Many women had told him how wonderful it was and yet he had known they were talking about him rather than The Castle itself.

When they entered through the front door, Rosetta did not speak. She was looking round her, taking in the magnificent staircase with its exquisitely carved balustrade.

There was a huge medieval sculptured fireplace and beside it were regimental flags commemorating at least a dozen battles when Millbrooks had fought with distinction.

The Marquis waited until Gordon and Henry had dismounted and their horses taken away by grooms.

"Welcome to my Castle," the Marquis intoned, "but before luncheon I think we all need a drink."

There was champagne waiting for them in one of the most beautiful drawing rooms Rosetta had ever seen.

The furniture was all French and the pictures were mostly by famous French artists.

There was a long glass-topped table in front of one window and Rosetta gave a gasp of delight when she saw it contained some of the snuffboxes she had been told the Marquis had in his collection.

"I think the French ones are beautiful," she sighed, "but the Russian are unique! And you are so lucky to own those boxes, which must have been popular in China and the East before the Europeans had even heard of them."

The Marquis thought it quite extraordinary, seeing how young she was, that she knew so much about so many different subjects.

After a delicious luncheon, the Marquis started to take them round some of the rooms in The Castle.

Again he found it almost impossible to believe that someone so young should know so much about pictures and furniture.

When later on in the afternoon he opened the door into the library, Rosetta gave a cry of delight.

"I have never seen a more magnificent library," she exclaimed, "or one that housed so many books! Have you read them all?"

The Marquis's eyes twinkled.

"Not entirely, I still need a few years before I catch up with you. I am sure that you will tell me you have read more books than I have, Dolina."

"As you are older than me, you should have read more than I have," retorted Rosetta. "These are fantastic and beautifully arranged in your library."

The Marquis reflected again with a slight feeling of pique that she was far more interested in his library than in its owner.

In fact, he had great difficulty in persuading Rosetta that there were other rooms he wished her to see before tea.

"Could I just slip back into the library before we leave?" Rosetta begged. "I see you have a Shakespeare Folio which I thought was only in the British Museum."

She talked of books until they reached the drawing room where tea was arranged for them.

The Marquis recognised that no other woman he had taken round The Castle had praised his possessions rather than himself.

He did notice that Gordon and Henry were almost tongue-tied by everything they saw and, as he felt that they were being somewhat neglected, he suggested,

"As soon as tea is finished, I have something quite different to show you that, I do believe, you will find as absorbing as your sister finds my other collections."

"What can it be?" Gordon asked.

Before the Marquis could speak, Henry cried,

"I know! You are going to show us your horses. I was afraid we might go home without seeing them."

"Of course you are going to see them, but I kept them until last because I thought that you would find them more enchanting than anything inside The Castle."

"Now you are making it impossible for me to say I want to go back to the library," protested Rosetta.

"It's for you to choose, Dolina," the Marquis added.

She smiled at him.

"You will know the answer already. Although The Castle is fantastic, Shakespeare can wait and I do want to see your horses too."

They all laughed and the Marquis thought that once again she was completely unlike anything he might have expected.

The stables were as magnificent as The Castle.

Gordon was promising himself that the moment they made any money from the Racecourse he would spend it in copying the Marquis's stables.

The horses themselves, as Rosetta anticipated, were sensational and she thought it would be very difficult for anyone to own a better collection.

There were far more of them than she or Gordon had expected and the Marquis admitted that he had been extremely extravagant lately.

"I have not only paid a large sum for my new team of horses," he told Rosetta, "but I mentioned the collection of exceptionally fine horses I was lucky enough to be able to buy before they were put up for auction."

"Yes, we do remember."

"Well, they were delivered this afternoon."

The Marquis grinned before he added,

"I hope you will approve of my extravagance."

He then led them to a stable at the far end of the yard, explaining that he had built it recently with every up-to-date gadget.

The new mangers and the way water was provided were most interesting to Gordon, but Rosetta was stunned by the horses themselves.

Never in her life had she seen a finer collection of such majestic thoroughbreds. They were so amazing to look at that they might have stepped out of a picture book.

"You need a Stubbs to paint them all and do them justice," she said in an awed voice.

"I thought they would please you, Dolina."

"They are absolutely and completely wonderful!" she enthused. "In fact there are no words to describe how splendid they are."

She walked from stall to stall talking to the horses and the Marquis mused that an artist would not only want to paint the horses but the beautiful woman admiring them.

"They are really a superb collection," said Gordon. "No man could be luckier than you, Euan."

"The only difficulty," Henry chimed in, "is that you have to decide which one to ride. To be fair, as they are all as good as each another, you will have to ride them one after another, which I reckon should take you a whole day at the very least!"

"It's an idea, but I actually have a better one," the Marquis laughed, "as you are admiring my horses so much and as I have greatly enjoyed staying with you at The Hall, I suggest, if you will have me, that I come back with you tonight, and tomorrow we all go riding together on my new horses. Not on the Racecourse, but over my land, which I think you will find almost as interesting as The Castle."

Before Gordon could speak, as he was taken aback by the invitation, Rosetta said,

"It's the most marvellous present you could give us, and thank you, thank you, Euan. I would rather ride one of your new horses than fly to the moon!"

"Then you shall ride the very best of them and now I suggest we go back to The Hall and you can tell me while we are driving there which horse is your special choice for tomorrow morning."

"I know which one I would love to have," Rosetta replied before either of the men could speak. "It's that one I believe should be named 'Horizon'."

The Marquis looked at her in surprise.

"I don't think I have heard that name used before," he murmured.

"I think it's a good name for a horse and for all of us. You have swept away so much darkness and given us an horizon to a new world that we fervently believe will be very different from what it has been in the past."

"Thank you," the Marquis bowed. "I think that is the nicest compliment I have ever received."

"You should be the best judge of that," she retorted.

The Marquis knew that she was teasing him.

Then they all returned to The Castle, having given instructions to one of the grooms to attach another team to the chaise.

"I cannot believe," Rosetta sighed, "they are better than those who brought us here."

"Perhaps no better, but old friends. I am sure that you of all people, Dolina, would not want them to feel that their noses have been put out of joint! The new arrivals are perhaps a little faster than they are."

Rosetta laughed.

"Now you are talking in a language that I can really understand. I am always afraid that my horses will feel neglected or they will feel I love and admire a new arrival more than I love them."

The Marquis thought it very touching that she cared so much for animals.

Some of the beauties he had pursued in London had ridden in Rotten Row simply because they wanted to show themselves off and they had little affection for their horses and nor did they worry about how they were cared for.

It seemed extraordinary to him that this girl, who has been acclaimed as a beauty, should have such affection for everything countrified.

He had not missed the way that she had admired the flowers that filled the drawing room.

He had seen her hand as she softly touched a rose or an orchid and, as they walked back through the garden, she was not thinking about him, she was concentrating on a bed of rose bushes that had always delighted him even as a small boy.

They had not hurried back into The Castle.

The chaise was waiting for them outside the front door and the Marquis was giving instructions to his valet to follow him with his clothes.

Gordon turned to Rosetta,

"I can only hope that Mrs. Barnes will excel herself tonight as she did last night."

"I am sure she will do her best," Rosetta said softly. "But I suggest you and Henry ride back the quick way over the fields. It will give her advance warning and, if there is anything extra she needs, she has time to order it."

"Of course and we might have thought of it on the way here, but we had to keep a little way behind, otherwise we would have had your dust in our eyes."

"If you go home across the fields, you will be back long before we are along all those twisting lanes."

When the Marquis had finished giving his orders, he found Rosetta alone.

"Where have Gordon and Henry gone?" he asked. "Don't tell me they have returned to the stables for another look at my horses."

"No, they have ridden home to make sure that the cook has something for our dinner. An unexpected guest, especially one as distinguished as you, causes a commotion in the kitchen!"

"I had not thought of that," the Marquis confessed.

He turned to his butler and instructed him,

"I will take with me that *pâté de foie-gras*, which I brought from London and which I have not yet sampled, together with a case of my best champagne."

"Very good, my Lord."

"That is so kind," Rosetta said as they walked down the front steps. "Men usually think that good food grows on gooseberry bushes and don't realise it requires a great deal of thought and hard work before it goes on the table."

"Do you ever find time to think about yourself?" the Marquis asked. "You always seem to think of others."

"I try to because so many of them are not happy in their lives. Therefore any kindness, however small, does give them pleasure."

"You are quite right, Dolina, but I have a feeling you are telling me in a roundabout and tactful way that I am selfish and too interested in myself."

"I am doing nothing of the sort, Euan. You have been exceedingly kind to us, and I am merely trying to help Gordon and Henry because they have been so desperately worried and had no one to help or care for them."

"They have you," the Marquis commented.

Rosetta realised that once again she had made a mistake, but she managed to avoid replying because they had now reached the chaise, drawn by a new team of, to her delight, white horses.

"How pretty they look!" she exclaimed.

"I thought you would like them, but I warn you they are getting on a bit and are not as fast as another team I own and they cannot compete with the new ones."

"There is no need for us to hurry."

The Marquis glanced at her.

"That is not a compliment to me as I first thought. You are still thinking of the cook!"

"Now you are reading my thoughts. I cannot think of any reason why I should worry about you."

"I can think of a lot of reasons why you should!"

As he was speaking, he picked up the reins.

He was thinking that there was a great deal he had to say to her.

It would be a challenge because she had made it clear that she had found The Castle and his horses more stimulating than he was.

He was wondering what she would say if he tried to kiss her and now he thought about it, it was something he had wanted to do ever since he had first seen her.

Yet he had been perceptively aware that it had never entered her mind that he wished to do so.

'Why is she so different?' he asked himself. 'Why does she not want me to be closer to her than I have been at meals? Why does she not look at me with that invitation in her eyes I have seen in so many other women? Why is she not excited by me as a man?'

All these questions were rushing through his mind again, but he had no answer to any of them.

Then he knew that, sitting beside him with her eyes on his team, she had made no effort to move closer so that her arm touched his or, as so many other women had done, put out a hand to rest on his knee.

"What are you thinking about?" he asked almost sharply.

There was a pause before Rosetta admitted,

"I was just thinking how wonderful The Castle is, but it is sad that so few people can see it."

The Marquis turned to look at her in surprise.

"What on earth do you mean by that?" he asked. "I often have friends down from London and those working on the estate come to The Castle from time to time."

"A mere handful of people, but The Castle is filled with so much beauty and all the achievements of those who lived hundreds of years ago."

"Are you really suggesting," the Marquis demanded incredulously, "that I should allow *the hoi polloi* to walk over my Castle?"

"No, not exactly. I merely thought that on special occasions and for rather special people, like those who are collecting for charity, it would be a joy and thrill if they could see all I have seen today, which I know is unique in the whole of England."

The Marquis was silent as he drove on and then he thundered,

"Supposing they steal some of the treasures I am lucky enough to own?

"It is a question of proper organisation. You would have guides in every room they visit who would keep an eye on anyone who might want to slip something into their pockets. And you would not tempt them unnecessarily by leaving the snuffbox cabinets unlocked."

After a while the Marquis muttered,

"You certainly put new ideas into my mind. At the same time, I cannot help thinking you are reproaching me for not thinking of them myself."

Rosetta smiled.

"I think actually you have been enjoying yourself as every man is entitled to do. But sooner or later you will want to spend much more time in your beautiful Palace, for there is no other word to describe it, and if people want to come to bow to you, can you really refuse them?"

The Marquis looked quizzically at Rosetta.

"You know, Dolina, you scare me. I am not going to listen to you any longer. I want to treat you as if you were just an ordinary beautiful woman, who should now be talking to me about love and what she feels about me."

He did not look at Rosetta and yet he sensed that she turned to stare at him.

He was quite certain she was completely surprised at what he had said to her.

But surely, he told himself, she has had men in London talking to her about love since the first moment she appeared there.

Then he told himself that it must be a pose.

Of course she had had thousands of compliments.

Doubtless a great number of young men had tried to kiss her and asked her to marry them.

No woman could be as beautiful as she was and go unnoticed.

He had heard all about her in London, but because they had never met, it had not occurred to him that she was different from other young women, who would invariably pursue him for his title or they wanted him to make love to them.

'I just don't understand her,' the Marquis thought as they drove on.

It really annoyed him as he believed that in his long experience he had met women of every type and so often they had turned out to behave exactly as the woman before her and the one before that.

He was driving through a small village that looked somewhat forlorn when Rosetta remarked,

"I am sorry if you think I have been rude or if I have offended you. It's only that you have so much and so many people have so little, that I was trying somehow to help both you and them."

She spoke humbly and the Marquis thought once again that this was unexpected.

He had never known a woman who could apologise so fully for what she had said or done.

"You have not said anything to apologise for," he replied. "You have merely made me think in a way I have not thought before. You are quite right and it is an issue I should have confronted."

"I expect a great number of people would think I was interfering and being tiresome, but I just cannot help saying what I think. My father has often told me it will get me into trouble sooner or later."

She knew as she spoke that she had made another mistake.

She was sure that the late Lord Waincliffe, who had sometimes visited her mother, would not have made that sort of comment.

But equally she remembered him as being a very charming man, who had always brought her presents.

He had also been very kind to her father when he retired and yet for some reason she had never understood he had never asked him or her up to The Hall.

It was only when she was older and heard people whispering about him and her mother that she realised her resemblance to Dolina might have been embarrassing.

'I must be more careful,' she told herself. 'I know I will say something to make the Marquis suspicious that we are deceiving him.'

They drove on in silence for a little while and then the Marquis asked her,

"Have you enjoyed yourself today? What will you remember about it more than anything else?"

Rosetta thought for a moment, wondering which of his many possessions she would choose as her favourite and then she replied,

"I think if I am absolutely honest with you what I will remember most about today is when we thanked the monk in his Chapel for making you more aware of how important it is not only to us but to many other people, that we should build a Racecourse."

The Marquis thought that this was just like her – to say something he did not expect.

He knew without asking that to her the monk was highly significant and she truly believed that it was he who made him agree that the Racecourse was really necessary.

"It will mean," he replied, "your brothers working very hard if it is to be a success. Although I will do what I can, I have many commitments I cannot avoid in London."

"Of course you have, Euan, but it will be exciting when you come down and see how far we have progressed and how thrilled everyone locally is at all we are doing."

She gave a murmur of satisfaction as she added,

"I am certain that they will all want to help – "

"I am quite sure you will make them do so. I think one person you should tell is the Lord Lieutenant. He is rather a bore, but it will be better to put him in the picture before he hears it from some mischief-maker or reads it in the newspaper."

"That would indeed make him extremely annoyed. We must persuade Gordon to ride over to see his Lordship tomorrow, before we start canvassing the local builders and carpenters for their help."

"I think," the Marquis advised, "you should go with Gordon. You are far more persuasive than he is and there is just a possibility that the Lord Lieutenant may think an influx of people into the neighbourhood could be harmful."

"Do you really think he would oppose us?" Rosetta asked in a frightened tone.

"No, I am only putting obstacles in your way," he said, "to see how you tackle them."

"You are now beginning to frighten *me*," Rosetta complained.

"It was very unkind of me. I am certain the Lord Lieutenant will be delighted that his County will evoke so much interest. Also I must tell you that when he resigns next year as he intends, Her Majesty has already suggested that I might accept the position – "

Rosetta clasped her hands together.

"Oh, that is marvellous news! Of course you will be a perfect Lord Lieutenant."

"There is one snag which unfortunately might just persuade Her Majesty to look elsewhere – "

"What is that?" Rosetta enquired.

"It is traditional that Lord Lieutenants are married!"

There was silence.

Then to his astonishment, Rosetta laughed.

"That will surely be no problem for you," she said. "According to newspaper reports, you are talked about as being seen with every beautiful woman in London. Surely one of them would make you a very suitable wife."

"Do you really think," the Marquis replied, "that I would marry anyone just to be Lord Lieutenant? If I do marry, I want to do so *for love*."

Because there was an angry note in his voice, she looked at him in amazement and then enquired,

"Despite everything they say about you, have you never really been in love?"

"No," the Marquis answered positively. "I don't want to talk about it, but as you have asked me, the answer is – *no, never*!"

He thought, as he spoke, that no one would believe him.

But it was the truth.

He had been enamoured, infatuated, and he had told a great number of females that he loved them.

But the truth was that he now knew that his heart had never been touched.

When he had left them, as invariably he did, he had never thought about them again.

Rosetta was silent and feeling surprised.

There had been so much talk about the Marquis.

Reports of his love affairs percolated down to the country, so that even the servants cracked jokes about him and some of the elderly folk called him a disgrace.

Yet, although she had found it hard to believe, she could understand in a way that his *affaires-de-coeur* never lasted long – almost before they had finished talking about one woman, there was another and yet another.

That merely increased the number of those who disapproved of him, who were shocked by all they heard.

Yet because he owned The Castle and because he was so handsome, he was naturally discussed by everyone, from the Lord Lieutenant's wife down to the customers in the little village shop.

Rosetta heard the gossip there, especially because the shopkeeper had two daughters – one was a housemaid at The Castle whilst the other one worked in the Marquis's kitchen in London.

It was therefore not extraordinary that their father always knew all that the Marquis was doing.

The village found the gossip more entertaining than anything they could read about in the newspapers.

But Rosetta had not imagined for one moment that he had never really been in love.

She knew now what he meant, as another woman might not have understood.

He was seeking, and it was rather strange that he had not yet found it, real love – *the real love* she had prayed would one day be hers.

They were still both silent when the Marquis turned in at the drive gates of The Hall.

Rosetta thought that Gordon and Henry would have been back some time by now and they would have told Barnes that the Marquis was staying for another night.

The Marquis drew the chaise to a standstill.

Rosetta was just about to say how quickly the team had brought them, when Barnes came running out.

Before opening the door of the chaise for Rosetta as she expected him to do, he went round to the other side and said to the Marquis,

"A man's just arrived, my Lord, from The Castle to say your aunt, the Countess of Wentworth, be arriving this evening. Her Ladyship says she has to see you. She says it's very important, my Lord."

The Marquis gave a deep sigh.

"That means I must return immediately. I knew my aunt was in trouble, but I did not expect her to descend on me without any warning."

"Then you must go to her at once," said Rosetta.

"Please apologise to your brothers on my behalf and tell them I will be rather late for dinner."

"I will tell them, Euan."

"And don't forget to talk to them about informing the Lord Lieutenant of our plans."

"Of course I will tell them and I do hope your aunt has not brought you bad news."

"I expect it's a problem I will have to solve."

Rosetta then stepped out of the chaise and closed the door behind her.

Now she held out her hand, saying,

"Thank you, thank you, Euan, for a very wonderful and exciting day."

"And thank you for being so beautiful! I will see you later."

He spoke in a voice he had never used to her before and, as their eyes met, it was impossible to look away.

With difficulty the Marquis lifted up the reins.

As Rosetta stepped back, she added,

"I will pray it's not as bad as you fear."

The Marquis did not answer, he only smiled at her.

Then raising his hat he turned his team round and he had started down the drive before Rosetta even moved.

With an effort she walked into the house.

She went to the study where she knew she would find Gordon and Henry.

As she came in, Gordon asked her,

"Where is the Marquis?"

"He has gone back to The Castle. I expect Barnes told you that his aunt is arriving unexpectedly this evening and wants to see him urgently."

"Thank God he will not be here!" cried Gordon.

Rosetta looked at him in surprise.

Why?" she asked, "and what has happened?"

"Just before we arrived back," Gordon replied, "a messenger arrived from London."

He held up a letter and then Henry chipped in,

"We can hardly believe what it says."

Rosetta walked across the room nearer to them.

"What has happened? What is wrong?"

"Perhaps it will be all right now the Marquis is not here with you, but this is a letter from Dolina."

Gordon opened it as he spoke, as if he was looking at it again to be quite sure that he had not been mistaken.

"From Dolina! What can have happened? Has she discovered that I am impersonating her?"

"No, it is not that. But she says – well I will read it to you."

He held the letter up in front of him and read aloud,

"*You may be surprised that I am sending this letter by messenger, but I want to tell you that my engagement is being announced tomorrow to the Duc de Maréy.*

It will be in The Gazette and I am so sorry I have not been able to let you know before.

I am leaving today for France to meet his family and we hope to be married immediately.

I am afraid they will want it to be in France.

You may, of course, come over for it and I will let you know the exact date as soon as I have met my fiancé's mother and the rest of the family."

Gordon stopped reading and looked at Rosetta.

"It will be in the newspapers tomorrow," he said, as if he could hardly believe it himself.

There was a short pause before Rosetta exclaimed,

"Then I must disappear. You must tell the Marquis when he comes tomorrow that I went back to London as soon as I arrived home and I am leaving for Paris with my fiancé."

"Surely he will think it very strange that we did not mention it today or yesterday."

Rosetta thought for a moment and then suggested,

"You must explain it was the Duc who put it in the newspapers as soon as he had told his mother that he was engaged. And it had to be a dead secret until she knew."

Gordon gave a sigh of relief.

"I think the Marquis might believe that."

"We can only hope so, but now, if you will be kind enough to arrange for someone to take me, I will pack my clothes, which will not take long, and go home."

She crossed the room as she spoke and then she went very quietly out of the study, closing the door behind her.

CHAPTER SEVEN

The Marquis drove back to The Castle to find his aunt reclining on a sofa in the drawing room.

He knew even before she uttered a single word that she had come to see him about her son who was inevitably heavily in debt.

The Marquis had paid up for him at least half a dozen times and he anticipated that it would be the same trouble once again.

His aunt put out her hand rather weakly.

"It's delightful to see you, Euan, but I am in very bad trouble."

"I felt so, Aunt Harriet, when you sent for me."

"I am afraid that you will be very angry with dear Roddie, but once again he has signed a cheque, which has bounced and he owes nearly five thousand pounds!"

Her voice faded away as she said the last words.

"Have you spoken to him severely as I told you to do the last time?" the Marquis asked.

"I have spoken to him harshly and begged him on my knees, but he will gamble! It's the only life he enjoys."

"At his age," the Marquis said, "he ought to be after the young girls. And it's high time he was married."

"So who would marry him as he is now? He sits gambling at his Club until the early hours of the morning and however amusing the parties he is asked to, he will not go to them because he would rather gamble."

The Marquis had heard of this before, but he never expected it would happen to one of his relations.

"I really don't know what to do about Roddie – "

"Oh, please, please dearest Euan," she now begged, "don't let him go to prison. I am so afraid that is where he will end up."

"That would certainly be dreadful for the family, but we have to stop his stupid behaviour once and for all."

"How can you do so?" she asked helplessly.

It flashed through the Marquis's mind that if Dolina was here, she would know the answer – *she* always had the solution to every problem and so this was just the sort of conundrum she could solve.

He walked over to the window and gazed out at the fountains playing in the garden, their water shining like rainbows in the setting sun.

He wondered what Dolina would do.

Almost as if she was talking to him, he knew what he should now say.

He turned round to face his aunt.

"I am just thinking it out, Aunt Harriet, and I am almost certain that I have found a solution."

"Oh, Euan, if you could only do that, it would not only stop me worrying but make me feel happy again. It's so long time since I have felt happy."

"You are not to make yourself unhappy over him."

"How can I be anything else?"

"Now listen, Aunt Harriet – "

He was visualising Dolina and her solution to this problem, as he began slowly,

"I will pay up again for him, but on one condition and it is irreversible."

"What is that?" his aunt asked plaintively.

"Roddie has to go abroad immediately to study the people of foreign countries he has never been to before," the Marquis stipulated, "starting with Nepal."

"That is a long way away."

"As far as I know, there is no gambling in Nepal and I feel sure he will become interested in something entirely different from anything he has done before."

"I see your point, Euan, but will Roddie go? You know how obstinate he can be."

"We will make it clear to him that I will not pay his debts until he is on the high seas. I will make sure he will be unable to leave the ship until he reaches India."

"Which will undoubtedly take a very long time, as the canal they talk so much about is not yet open."

"And I will make certain that he is not allowed to play cards or anything else for money on board the ship. If he breaks my rules, then I will not pay up and when he returns to England, if he does return, he will be arrested."

"It sounds rather frightening," she murmured.

"I intend to frighten him, Aunt Harriet, he is not so stupid as to get himself put into prison. You know as well as I do that he is banking on me not wanting a scandal that would damage the family name."

Aunt Harriet thought it over and then she said,

"I think your idea is right. We cannot go on as we are. I feel terribly upset to come and ask you again, dear Euan, to save Roddie from himself."

"What I suggest now, Aunt Harriet, is that you go to bed and my butler will bring you up a delicious supper. Tomorrow we will talk this over again and I expect you will want to tell Roddie about my decision."

"Yes, I must tell him, and you must put in writing exactly what he has to do and how the only way he can avoid being arrested is to leave England."

"I will arrange all that for you. All I want you to do now is to have a nice rest and then go home and be very firm with Roddie."

"How can I ever thank you for being so kind, but as you say, this cannot go on, and unless we do something desperate like sending him to Nepal, he will only run up even more huge gambling debts."

Aunt Harriet spoke despairingly and the Marquis reflected that the trouble with Roddie was that he had been spoilt as a child.

He was, however, not too far off from succeeding to the Earldom of Wendover.

His elder brother, the present Earl, had never been strong and there was every likelihood that he would not live very long and the Marquis realised that, if Roddie came into the title, he would merely continue gambling until there was nothing left.

He helped his aunt to her feet and he made her take his arm as she walked unsteadily towards the door.

"I cried all last night," she sighed, "so I am glad now I have seen you and you have been so good to me. Now I will look forward a good night's sleep."

"You are not to worry, Aunt Harriet. Just leave everything to me, but Roddie must do as he is told. I will find out first thing tomorrow morning the name of the next ship leaving for India and I promise you he will be on it."

"You are so kind, so very very kind, Euan."

The Marquis helped her up to her bedroom and sent for her maid.

Then he hurriedly changed into his evening clothes, knowing that he would be a little late for dinner with the Waincliffes.

But at least he would not have to dine alone and he would be able to talk to Dolina.

He wanted to tell her all about the problem and see if she would have solved it in the same way and anyway he felt sure she was guiding him in the right direction.

When he was dressed, he went again to his aunt's room to find her cosily in bed and she was actually smiling as he walked towards her.

"You look so smart, dear Euan," she sighed. "How I wish Roddie was like you."

"I am sure Roddie, when he pulls himself together and stops gambling, will be a credit to you and the whole family, but you have to be firm with him as I intend to be."

"You always say the right thing. I was afraid that, as you have been so kind in the past, you would feel that this time Roddie should fend for himself. You know what that would mean?"

"You are not to think about it. Just remember that I am acting as Fairy Godfather for the last time and Roddie must realise that he has to pull himself together. If he does not do as he is told, he will be unable to return to England and will be a penniless outcast for the rest of his life."

Aunt Harriet made a little murmur of agreement.

The Marquis bent forward and kissed her.

"That is how we have to frighten him and I am sure he will find there is nothing he can do but obey us."

"Thank you again for everything, dearest Euan."

"We will talk again tomorrow morning, but now you must rest, Aunt Harriet."

The Marquis left her and hurried downstairs.

His horse was waiting outside the front door.

He had thought, although it seemed ridiculous to be riding in his evening clothes, that he would get to The Hall much quicker than if he drove through the twisting roads.

He rode off, hoping that Dolina would approve of what he had done.

It was, he was now musing, the only sensible way he could cure Roddie of his disastrous gambling.

*

When he arrived at The Hall, he was shown into the study, where Gordon and Henry were waiting for him.

"Please forgive me if I am late," the Marquis said as he entered.

"But you are not," Henry replied. "It's only five minutes past nine o'clock and I think it is wonderful of you to have gone all the way home and then to ride back again dressed in your best."

The Marquis laughed.

"It was much quicker than coming by road. I had one of my best horses and we arrived in record time."

"Another record!" Gordon exclaimed. "We must certainly drink to that."

He handed the Marquis a glass of champagne and then he asked,

"Where is your sister? I cannot believe she is late and I have something important to tell her."

There was a rather uncomfortable silence and then Gordon replied,

"Actually we have had somewhat of a drama here."

"A drama? What do you mean?"

"We have just been told that the Duc de Maréy is announcing his – and Dolina's engagement tomorrow in –

The Gazette. And they are immediately leaving for France – to meet his family."

Gordon stumbled over his words and he was aware the Marquis was staring at him as if he could not believe his ears.

There was a long silence until finally the Marquis enquired,

"Are you telling me that your sister is engaged to be married?"

"Apparently so, although it was a secret from us as well as everyone else," said Henry. "We are as astonished as you are that the Duc has put the announcement in *The Gazette* without even informing us."

Again there was an uncomfortable silence until the Marquis remarked sharply,

"I had no idea that your sister was engaged. In fact, as she seemed so happy in the country and was going to help us with the Racecourse, I did not think that there was a man in her life."

"Nor did we," the brothers chorused. "We were surprised, but naturally we want her to be happy."

The Marquis drank his champagne.

Again no one spoke.

It was a relief when the door opened and Barnes announced,

"Dinner is served, my Lord."

They went into the dining room, but it was difficult to carry on a conversation.

The Marquis was obviously upset and he made no effort to be witty and amusing as he had been the previous evening.

Dinner seemed to drag on and on.

The two brothers were desperately afraid that the Marquis would announce that he was no longer interested in the Racecourse.

As soon as dinner was finished, the Marquis said he must go back to his aunt.

"She is very worried about her son," he explained, "and I promised to discuss it with her tonight."

"Of course we understand," said Gordon. "Are we meeting again tomorrow to look at the Racecourse?"

It was a very important question.

He crossed his fingers waiting for the Marquis's answer.

There was an ominous pause before the Marquis responded,

"As my aunt is staying with me, I am not certain when she is leaving. I will let you know when I am free."

"Thank you, thank you very much, Euan. We were thinking later in the day of going over to meet the Lord Lieutenant."

"I had not forgotten."

The Marquis was walking towards the front door as he spoke and the brothers saw that he hurried to his horse. He had told Barnes to have it brought round as soon as dinner was finished.

He mounted and then, raising his hat, he rode away without saying anything more.

As he disappeared out of sight, Gordon sighed,

"If you ask me, I think that means the end of the Racecourse."

"I agree," added Henry, "he was obviously upset that Dolina was not with us."

The brothers walked back to the drawing room and then Henry suggested,

"Suppose we tell him that it was not Dolina who was helping us, but the daughter of Professor Stourton?"

"Do you really think he would ever forgive us for deceiving him? I think if we do that, he would never trust us again and we can forget the Racecourse right away."

"If we do go ahead with it," replied Henry, "he will doubtless see Rosetta eventually, even if it's by chance."

"By that time he will have forgotten about Dolina and what she looks like," Gordon said optimistically. "If you ask me the whole thing is finished, *absolutely finished*, and we are back where we started, wondering how either of us can find a penny to bless ourselves with!"

He threw himself down into an armchair and Henry walked to the window.

Neither of them said anything further.

It was as if the night was closing in on them.

*

Riding home, the Marquis was feeling the same.

He was furious that Dolina had never mentioned this Duc to him.

He had not the slightest idea that she intended to be married and leave Waincliffe Hall, presumably for ever.

He admitted now that he had found her fascinating, amusing and although he had always shied away from the word – *irresistible*.

Because they had been planning far ahead, he had never for a moment thought that he might lose her.

Or that she could possibly disappear from his life in the same abrupt way as she had entered it.

'I have lost her,' he muttered to himself angrily.

Then he knew that, although he had hidden it from everyone else and even from himself, he had fallen in love.

She was so beautiful that at times he felt she could not be human – but it was much more than just that.

It was the way she laughed, the way she teased him.

The way she had read his thoughts.

He could not imagine life without her.

It had never passed through his mind that she might leave him.

Or that there was another man in the background waiting to claim her as his wife and then spirit her away to another country.

'How could I have been such a fool?' the Marquis asked himself, 'as to plan my future interests around her? Now that she is no longer here, I feel as if the bottom has fallen out of my world and I really am entirely alone.'

He now admitted to himself that he had been falling in love with her more and more each time they met.

If he was honest, he had agreed to the planning of the Racecourse merely because he would see more of her.

And even just because she wanted it!

He was prepared to give her the Racecourse as well as the moon and the stars.

He drew nearer and nearer to The Castle.

As he did so, he realised that, for the first time in his life, it was taking second place in his thoughts.

There was at this moment only Dolina, *Dolina*!

As he thought of her, he could hear the softness of her voice and the music of her laughter.

He could not put her bewitching quality into words.

He only knew that when she was near him, he felt as if he came alive!

He was so sure their vibrations touched each other, even though she had never looked at him in the way he wanted her to.

He had never put it into words, but he had felt it was just a question of time and then she would realise how important he was to her.

Just as he knew that she was everything to him.

'This is love, the love I have sought all my life *and now I have lost it.*'

The words seemed to be written in fire in front of his eyes as he arrived at The Castle.

As he dismounted, he wished he could somehow reach London before she left for France.

He would beg her, if necessary on his knees, to stay with him.

But he knew it was impossible.

As he walked into The Castle, he felt as if he was walking towards the guillotine.

*

Riding back to her home on Starlight which Gordon had insisted on lending her, Rosetta felt as if the door of a safe filled with treasures had been shut abruptly in her face.

She had never been so happy as she had been these last few days.

Not only seeing The Castle and talking about the Racecourse but just being with the Marquis.

She had been so prepared to hate him, because he neglected his people.

A nd, because she thought the stories about his love affairs in London were unpleasant, he did not behave as a Marquis of Millbrook should.

Yet when she was with him, it was impossible not to forgive him.

Impossible not to find that he was very different in every way from the man she had envisioned.

She had been thrilled and delighted he had listened to all she had to say and agree to finance the Racecourse.

She had enjoyed more than anything else the way they had duelled with each other in words.

She had managed not only to make him laugh but to think what she wanted him to think.

It had all been fascinating and tantalising.

She had known, when she woke in the morning, she was instantly thinking of the Marquis and wondering how soon she would be seeing him again.

'I have been stupid enough to fall in love,' she told herself frantically. 'Now I have to avoid him and never speak to him again.'

She felt as if the very thought of it drew a darkness over the setting sun.

It even made the flowers in her garden appear faded and not as beautiful as when she had left them.

Her father, however, was delighted to see her.

"It's so nice to have you back, my dear," he said, "although your aunt is looking after me very well. There is a most interesting book she has been reading to me, which I wish to discuss with you when you have the time."

"I have plenty of time for you now, Papa."

Her father looked at her enquiringly and then she explained to him about the Racecourse.

"So the Marquis is really going to pay for it?"

"He has promised he will," replied Rosetta, "and, of course, Lord Waincliffe and his brother are thrilled."

"I expect they are, from what I hear they are almost penniless and The Hall is falling down on their heads."

"Quite a number of ceilings have already fallen in and I cannot imagine how they will ever be able to pay for repairs unless, as they hope, the Racecourse makes them a lot of money."

"It certainly will if it ever materialises, but I expect it will take time and these grandiose ideas often come to nothing."

It was what Rosetta was afraid of, but she did not say so to her father.

She went to the kitchen where, Betty, their maid, was delighted she had come home.

"I've missed you, Miss Rosetta," she said, "and I tells you it's much too far for me to walk to the village to get the food for the Master. So I'm real glad you be back and that's the truth."

"I will bring all you will need tomorrow morning," Rosetta promised. "But Papa seems in good health and you know he enjoys your cooking far more than mine."

"Now you're flatterin' me, miss. You be a brilliant cook for sure or I wouldn't be a-sayin' it."

"Thank you, Betty."

Rosetta walked slowly up to her room.

Gazing out of the window, she wondered what was happening at The Hall.

Would the Marquis be annoyed she was not there when he returned in the evening? Or would he be content to talk to the boys about the Racecourse without her?

'*I love him,*' she whispered into the twilight.

As far as she was concerned, she had left her heart at The Hall.

*

Dinner was quite a pleasant meal with her father discussing a new book that had just been published. As it was a history of Scotland, it was as interesting to Rosetta as it was to him. It described many of the great castles lying North of the border.

When they talked about castles, she could not help thinking that no castle could be as beautiful or as exciting and enchanting as the one belonging to the Marquis.

'Perhaps I will never see it again,' she mused to herself, 'unless he does as I asked him and opens the doors to the public.' She thought, if he did so, she would be one of the first to cross the threshold as a tourist.

Then she was forced to remind herself that she had to hide from him – maybe for two or three years until he had forgotten her.

That, of course, he would find quite easy to do if he believed she was living in France as the wife of the Duc.

Because her father was almost an invalid, he went to bed early and so did her aunt.

Rosetta stayed in the garden for some time and then because the beauty of the moon and the stars hurt her, she felt that she should retire to bed.

But she knew it would be impossible to sleep when she was thinking of the Marquis.

She now wanted, as she had never wanted anything before, to be with him – to talk to him, to listen to him and to hear him laugh.

'I love him, I love him,' she told the stars over and over again.

Then she turned round to walk back to the house, but, because she knew she would not sleep, she hesitated.

She remembered that tomorrow at any rate it would be dangerous for her to ride, just in case by any chance she came into contact with the Marquis.

It had not struck her before how difficult it would be to hide from him, especially if he rode as much as he did at The Castle.

Yet in the past he had always returned to London after just a short visit.

Then Rosetta told herself she was being silly.

Of course he would go back to the beautiful women who were missing him and who kept the village tongues wagging.

It was easy to say that, but she would not be able to ride as she usually did if he was also out riding.

She was now feeling agitated, so she went to her horse's stall. He was obviously pleased to see her and he nuzzled against her as she patted him.

"Have you missed me, Atlas? I am sure you have."

She felt guilty because she had enjoyed riding the other horses, especially the Marquis's and Starlight.

"You are mine, Atlas" she muttered, "and now you have to help me. I need your help more than I have ever needed anything before."

She saddled him and then without bothering about her dress, she mounted him.

Then she rode out of the garden and onto the land outside.

The moon was now high in the sky and the stars were twinkling cheekily at her.

She felt all she needed now was help and guidance.

The only person in the world she could turn to who would understand was the monk.

She had gone to him so many times in the past, in fact, whenever she felt lonely, unhappy or worried.

Somehow, when she had prayed, he had helped her and she had known the answer to the questions in the back of her mind.

'I will go to him now,' she decided. 'I will tell him I am in love and only he will make me understand that it's only a dream that can never become reality.'

Once again, she told herself that the Marquis would soon forget her now she was no longer there.

She had amused him, she had interested him.

But, when he returned to London and the glittering parties at Marlborough House, he would never think of her again.

As she told herself that, it was as if a knife pieced her heart. She felt the agony of it was more intense than anything she had ever known.

She did not hurry, but rode across the fields and came to the beginning of Monkswood.

She did not enter it the way she had done when the Marquis had followed her – then she had ridden along the path that went into the very centre of the wood.

Now she rode round outside the wood because she did not want to have to guide Atlas in the darkness.

She wanted to keep in the moonlight until she was near to the Chapel and could reach it easily.

Her well-trained horse would stay in the field and wait for her.

She found the place she had so often visited before.

Having tied the reins together over his neck, she left Atlas free to eat the grass, knowing he could not go far. She had only to whistle and then he would come galloping up to her.

"I will not be long," she said as she patted his neck.

Then she walked into the wood.

She knew the way so well that even in the darkness she did not stumble in the undergrowth.

She walked along a path she had made herself that led to the centre of the wood where the Chapel was.

Then, suddenly to her great astonishment just ahead of her, there was a light.

She stopped and wondered what it could be.

Then she realised it was a fire. It was quite a small one, but she could see it between the trees.

Someone had lit a fire near the pool and the Chapel and for a moment she wondered who it could possibly be.

Then she thought it must be poachers – Gordon had complained about them and so had the Marquis. Perhaps the men were setting traps and that would certainly annoy the joint owners of the wood.

Moving very slowly, so that she would not make a noise and attract attention, she moved from tree to tree.

Once she was close enough, she could see the fire burning brightly beside the pool.

It illuminated both the flowers growing round the pool and, to her great surprise, a number of men sitting on the ground around it.

She could see their heads very clearly.

She counted ten of them.

Ten men!

It seemed incredible that they should be poaching in such a large number and anyway it was too early in the year for the pheasants.

Now she could hear their voices and they sounded different to the villagers.

They were certainly not local men and she had a suspicion, although she was not at all sure, that they had Cockney accents.

Creeping a little nearer, but keeping well behind the trees, she moved forward.

Now she could hear what they were saying –

"There be no 'urry," one of the men said in a very rough voice. "If we waits till nigh on midnight, there be no one about as I finds out last night."

"I 'opes they didn't see you?" one of the other men asked.

"No, course not, them stables be so big you can 'ide an army in 'em."

Another man laughed.

"Let's 'ope there won't be no army there tonight."

"Don't worry," the first man replied. "I sees 'im goin' orf to bed soon after nine and I watches the lights in the top rooms and they goes orf 'bout ten o'clock."

"What about them grooms who be there at night?" another man enquired. "I 'ears in all them smart stables there be a nightwatchman."

"I 'ears that too," another chimed in. "But if they be the young 'uns and unmarried they sleeps like babies and if they do wake, we'll deal with 'em quick enough."

The man who had spoken first came back,

"The one I 'ears last night were a-snorin' like a grampus!"

They laughed and then another man scoffed,

"Would you know a grampus if you saw one?"

"I'd know 'im if 'e be as good as them 'orses," came the answer. "And don't forget we've got to get 'em to Southampton as quick as we can. Once they be out of the

145

country, the money'll be in our pockets. And who's to know we've taken 'em away?"

"Who indeed and a pretty price the Count be payin' for 'em."

"Them foreigners 'as more money than us and you can bet 'e'll be winnin' big prizes at the races at Paris and other places on yon Continent."

"Now what you've got to do," the first man said, "instead of all this talk, be to make real sure your gun be workin', but don't kill 'em unless you 'as to. Aim for their arms or their legs and they'll not be able to stop us takin' them 'orses. And there won't be no hue and cry after us if none be dead."

"That be true enough. I knows we be good shots."

"The most important thing," one added, "be to get them 'orses away afore any of 'em knows just what's goin' on!"

"That be exactly what we be a-goin' to do. When they wakes in the mornin', them 'orses won't be there and they'll 'ave no idea where they be gorn to!"

"Then 'is Nibs can go back to 'is pretty ladies – and *them* won't be runnin' away from 'im!"

There was laughter and one of them made a remark so vulgar that Rosetta did not want to hear it.

She knew she had heard enough.

What she must do urgently and *at once* was to warn the Marquis as soon as she possibly could.

Creeping back very slowly, she knew what would happen if they had the slightest suspicion they had been overheard – the men would either take her prisoner or kill her to stop her talking.

The way she had come into the wood had seemed very easy when she had first walked along it.

Now it seemed an eternity before, hardly daring to breathe, she reached the place where she had left Atlas.

He was cropping the grass and she ran towards him.

Then she rode away.

It was some distance before she finally turned and headed for The Castle.

She rode as fast as she could, forcing Atlas into a gallop until they reached the orchard and then the garden.

She rode frantically across the lawn.

And then she turned round the corner of the house towards the front door.

Everything was very quiet, but she knew that there would be a night footman on duty in the hall.

She beat her fists on the door.

When the footman opened it, she pushed her way in before she spoke.

"Wake every man in the house and the stables," she cried breathlessly, "as quick as you can. Thieves are going to steal the horses that arrived this afternoon!"

Even as she spoke, she started to climb the stairs.

"I will warn his Lordship," she shouted, "but hurry, hurry and rouse the men!"

The footman had obviously seen her before and she heard him running across the hall and under the staircase as she reached the landing.

She tore along the corridor.

Fortunately, when the Marquis had been showing her and the boys round the Castle, he had taken them into his own room.

He had told them that all the Marquises had always slept there and it was a most impressive bedroom.

Looking at the enormous four-poster bed with its red velvet curtains and embroidered heraldry of the family, Rosetta had thought that he was right.

As she pulled open the door, she was afraid for a moment that it might be locked.

But it was not.

Now she could see that the Marquis was not asleep, but sitting up in bed reading a book.

She was not to know until later that he had tried to sleep, but had found it impossible because he was thinking about her, so he had thought instead he would read until he was really tired and then fall asleep through exhaustion.

As it was, when Rosetta ran to the end of his bed, he stared at her in utter astonishment.

He thought he must be dreaming.

"There are ten ruffians planning to steal your new horses and sell them overseas," she called out anxiously.

It was hard to speak clearly, because she had run up the stairs so quickly.

The Marquis could only stare at her.

"They are coming here at midnight," she screamed. "They have guns and will shoot at your men if they try to prevent them from taking the horses."

"How do you – know this?" the Marquis asked her, feeling bewildered.

For a moment, he found it difficult to take in what she was saying, because in the candlelight she looked so indescribably lovely.

It was almost impossible to believe she was there.

It could *not* be true.

"I was going to the Chapel," she said in a breathless little voice, "and they were sitting there in the wood beside the pool. When I heard what they said – I knew I had to warn you."

"Tell the footman in the hall to rouse the servants in the house," instructed the Marquis, "while I dress."

"I have already told him to do so. I will go to the window while you dress."

She walked across the room and pulled back the curtain over one of the windows."

The moonlight seemed almost to envelope her.

She was still breathless from running so quickly up the stairs and the strange sensation she had felt in her heart as she saw the Marquis sitting up in bed was still with her.

Now she could hear him moving about the room and opening a cupboard as he dressed and then he told her,

"Now you can turn round. You said the men were carrying guns?"

"Yes, and one said they were going to shoot anyone who interfered with them, not so as to kill, but to wound them in the arm or leg."

"Very well. I feel certain we have enough guns to compete with them."

"But you must hurry," urged Rosetta. "They said they would come at midnight and it must be getting near that by now."

As she spoke, she realised that the Marquis had already reached the door.

As she ran after him, he turned round and took her hand.

"I might have guessed that if there was trouble, you would save me!"

"It is what I am trying to do, but we must hurry."

The Marquis did not answer.

Still holding her hand, he hurried along the passage and they ran down the stairs together.

To her relief there were already half-a-dozen men in the hall. Some of them were scantily dressed and they had clearly come as soon as the footman had roused them.

"You will want guns, all of you," the Marquis said sharply, as he jumped down the last steps. "Hurry to the gun room and pick up a gun you can fire and don't worry about me. I have my revolver with me."

Rosetta saw he was carrying it in his other hand.

The men ran down the passage and for a moment the Marquis and Rosetta were alone in the hall.

"You must be very careful," she said. "I think they have come from London and are determined to take your horses to Southampton and sell them for a very large sum."

"I promise you they will not succeed!"

There was the sound of men running back from the gun room.

"You must stay here, Dolina," added the Marquis, "and I will come and tell you when it is all over."

"I am coming with you," Rosetta insisted. "You know the horses will be upset at the sound of shots. I will look after them and try to stop them being frightened."

The Marquis smiled and whispered,

"I might have known you would say something like that!"

There was no chance of saying anything else as the servants had now joined them.

Without giving any further orders, the Marquis ran towards the back of the house, followed by his staff.

He was holding tightly onto Rosetta's hand and did not relinquish it until they opened a door at the back of the kitchen.

She saw that they were now in a narrow path that led to the stables.

There was no one to be seen and the Marquis then turned round,

"Move silently in case someone is watching us and don't speak."

He went ahead, taking Rosetta's hand again.

They reached the door leading into the stable block.

It was then the Marquis started giving his orders.

Without waiting to listen, Rosetta slipped inside.

The horses she had seen that afternoon were, she thought, even finer than she remembered and she could quite understand any man who valued horseflesh wanting to own them.

Some were lying down and some were standing up and she went from stall to stall talking to them in a very quiet and reassuring voice.

She was aware that the Castle staff and the Marquis were now inside the stables.

However, she was more concerned with the horses and yet she could feel the tension rising.

Then quite suddenly, so that she started and so did the horses, there came the first shot from the Marquis's revolver.

It was followed by a scream and then a fusillade of shots that seemed to boom into the air and make everything seem terrifying and unreal.

The horses began rearing up at the noise and it was impossible for Rosetta to calm them.

Then, just as suddenly as the shooting had started, it stopped.

The Marquis went out into the yard and because she was curious, Rosetta could not help but glance through the door he had left open.

Then she could see there were ten men lying on the ground, groaning and swearing with fury.

Just as the thieves had intended to shoot anyone who interfered with them, they had been shot in the same way – either in the arm or the leg.

The horses behind her were trembling at the noise, but they were no longer rearing.

Rosetta could not resist going over to the door to see what was happening.

She heard the Marquis say,

"Put these creatures into the largest van we possess and drive them to the Police Station. Charge them with attempted burglary and tell the Inspector I will make a full statement in the morning."

"Very good, my Lord," a man replied, who Rosetta felt must be the Head Groom.

Other grooms now appeared, but the Marquis told them they must attend to the horses and he then sent four of his footmen with the van as well as the Head Groom.

"If there is any trouble from them," the Marquis ordered, "shoot them again!"

"We have already taken their weapons from them, my Lord," the butler reported.

"Good man," the Marquis replied.

The van started towards the gates at the end of the yard and as they passed by her, Rosetta she could hear the wounded men groaning and shouting inside.

The Marquis was thanking all his servants who had helped him so courageously.

"You have all been splendid. I now suggest we go back to the house and then whilst you bring me a bottle of champagne, open one for yourselves. We have won a great victory tonight and it is all due to Miss Dolina, who came to warn me that this outrage was about to happen."

"Then we'll drink her health, my Lord," the butler said.

"And drink your own as well."

They were delighted.

And then, taking Rosetta by the hand, the Marquis walked with her back to The Castle – not the way they had come, but through the front door.

They went into the Marquis's study and the butler brought in the champagne and poured it out for them.

The Marquis did not speak as Rosetta sat down in an armchair.

Finally when they were alone, the Marquis began,

"Now tell me why you are here, Dolina, and how you have been so incredibly brave as to save my horses?"

"I went to pray in the Chapel – "

"Why were you not in London, as I was told you were?" the Marquis asked.

Rosetta looked away from him and she then replied rather shyly,

"If I tell you the truth, perhaps you will be angry."

"Do you think I could *ever* be angry with you?"

There was a short silence and then she confessed,

"I am not, as you think – Dolina."

"Then *who* are you?"

"I am Rosetta Stourton and my father is Terence Stourton, Professor of Literature."

For a moment, the Marquis could hardly believe his ears.

"Apparently I look very like Dolina Waincliffe and I was asked by Gordon and Henry to pretend to be Dolina because she insisted on going to London and they were so anxious to persuade you to build the Racecourse, and, as you like pretty women, the boys believed that I would be useful in persuading you to help them."

"Which you most certainly did. Now, my darling, what are you going to do about *me*?"

Rosetta looked up at him and sighed,

"And now, Euan, to begin with, you will have be become used to calling me Rosetta and not Dolina."

For the first time he saw the look in her eyes he had so longed to see.

Very slowly, as if he was afraid of frightening her, he put his arms around her.

"I knew tonight, when I returned to The Hall and you were not there," he murmured, "that I love you as I have never loved anyone else. I was so desperate because I had lost you and, now you have come back to me, I will never ever let you go, *my Rosetta.*"

"Do you really mean it?" she asked. "I knew when I had to run away, I wanted to be with you always."

"Tell me what I want to hear – "

"I love you, Euan" Rosetta declared. "I love you as I have always wanted to love someone, but I am frightened I am not grand enough for you."

The Marquis gave a laugh.

"You are everything I ever wanted, and far grander to me than if you were the Queen."

He pulled her a little closer.

"I promise I will never lose you again."

He kissed her passionately, at the same time almost reverently as if he was afraid she might vanish into thin air.

As his kisses became more demanding and more fervent, Rosetta knew that they had found the love they had both sought.

"I love you. My God how I love you!" the Marquis sighed, "and this, my darling, is *real* love. I have said it before, but it has never been true, because it did not come from my heart. But I knew when you went out of my life, as I thought, that I could never be the same again."

"And I love you," Rosetta whispered to him. "I have never loved anyone because they always seemed so foolish and so dull. But you are wonderful and I love you as you love me, with my heart, my mind and my body."

The Marquis smiled.

"Only you could put it exactly as I would want to put it myself. I love you, my darling, and we will make the world a better place simply because we love each other."

He kissed her again and then he proposed,

"How soon will you marry me, my precious?"

"Whenever – you want me to," she answered.

"Then we will be married in my own Chapel, for which I do not need a Special Licence and I cannot wait any longer than tomorrow."

Rosetta laughed.

"What about your family?"

"They can hear about it afterwards, just as Gordon and Henry heard about Dolina when it was too late for them to do anything about it!"

Rosetta hesitated for a moment.

"Suppose that your family don't think I am grand enough for you."

"Do you honestly believe that anything anyone else thinks would matter to me? I have been looking for you ever since I can remember and believed you did not exist.

"I am not taking any chances. You will marry me tomorrow night and then we will go abroad to explore the places you have longed to see that I want to show you."

"That will be wonderful, Euan, but before we go can we tell the boys to go ahead with the Racecourse?"

"You would think of that right in the middle of my being, I reckoned, so unbelievably romantic!"

"I will be as romantic as you want me to be, but we have to tie up the ends. I am here in your arms because George and Henry wanted a Racecourse!"

The Marquis drew her closer.

"*The Winning Post is Love*," my darling Rosetta. "I will agree to anything you want – as long as you are mine."

Then he was kissing her wildly and fervently.

Her body seemed to melt into his.

Rosetta felt they were stepping through the gates of Heaven.

A Heaven in which the love they both sought was there waiting for them.

The love that came from God, was part of God and would be theirs for all Eternity.